MW01172108

Guilty Is Not Enough

Life of a Whistleblower

By

Greg Stallworth

CONTENTS

Acknowledgments

Greg Stallworth is a Playwright/Author of Stallworth Productions. As a Playwright Greg has produced over 25 stage productions. As an author he has written and published six books, most notably his book A Dream UNDENIED that was accepted into the 2021 Portland Multicultural Reading and Film Festival In addition to his recent acknowledgment Greg's stage play A Mother's Plea was accepted into the 2015 National Black Theatre Festival. Because of its success his production was converted into a film short. Greg has received numerous awards including the acceptance in the prestigious Playwrights on Parade Celebration. His stage play production titled A Black Father's Plea has been accepted into the 2023 Pacific Multicultural Reading and Film Festival. Greg's inspiration toward his God given literary gift is given to his wife Rose, his children along with the following supporters that include Curtis Shepard, David Livers, Maxwell Highsmith, Gail Woods, Martha Bonham and Reynard Cain.

Tracie Black

First of all, I would like to thank my mother for being the strong woman that she was and raising me to have the strength and courage to do anything I set my mind to do. She truly believed in me and has helped me through many trials and tribulations. She always gave great advice and never told me anything wrong. May she rest in heaven!!! I would like to give thanks to my wonderful children Tray, Travell and Lars. They have always supported everything that I have done as well as encourage me to do more. I truly appreciate their patience as I continue to explore new adventures. Without them, I wouldn't be the woman that I am today! Last, but not least, I would like to thank my Uncle Greg for being a great mentor and coaching me through this journey. He has helped me tremendously in several aspects of my life. Most importantly, I would like to thank him for this amazing opportunity and I look forward to collaborating again in the near future.

Introduction

What would you do if you arrived at work and received voice messages on your office phone about an alleged drug trafficking operation going on where you worked? What would you do if you have no knowledge to who is involved in this illegal operation? Guilty Is Not Enough brings a powerful story to light of the perils working in Corporate America where the stakes are high and the risk are subjectively higher. Imagine you are a very successful and respected corporate executive who is responsible for taking the corporation to Fortune 500 status. Aaron, very respectful and successful corporate executive caught in a vice between his loyalty to the corporation or reporting what he knows to the authorities. By going to law enforcement does Aaron take a chance of losing your job and more critically risk losing your life? What happens next is cathartic scenes of the most devastating turn of events one can encounter dealing with fear and anxiety. When Guilty Is not Enough speaks of Aaron, a corporate executive who helped his corporation receive the Fortune 500 award for being one of the nation's top financial companies. Shortly after receiving this prestigious award his corporation was investigated by the feds involving an international drug tracking ring involving the corporation. After a series of the most suspense acts of terror involving a murder for hire plot things take the most unbelievable twist from crime to justice. This story brings to extreme detail to the meaning of who can you trust.

Chapter 1

Aaron Williams, a neatly dressed African American Corporate Executive wearing a navy blue Brooks Brothers suit walks into the Pyramid Office Towers lobby enters the elevator ascending to the 17th floor. Arriving at the Remington Corporation offices, he adjusts his cherry red tie that sits neatly on his pearl white dress shirt. As he enters into the offices he is greeted by Camille, the Receptionist a very attractive woman of Hispanic descent speaking in a soft and pleasant voice.

"Good morning Aaron," says Camille.

"Good Morning Camille. Have I received any calls?" asks Aaron.

"Yes sir, I sent them to your voice mail," says Camille smiling. After thanking Camille, Aaron walks into his office and places his briefcase on his oak colored executive desk. Taking a seat in his black executive chair, Aaron notices that he has received an interoffice message on his phone from Robert Remington Sr., President and CEO of the Remington Corporation. As Aaron nervously presses the button on his phone and places it on speaker phone he waits for Mr. Remington to answer. After several rings Mr. Remington answers in a very spirited voice.

"Good morning Aaron, how are you this morning? I would like to see you in my office as soon as possible," says Remington. Hearing Mr. Remington's request, Aaron responds.

"I am on my way sir," says Aaron. Curious to why he wants to see him Aaron gets up from his chair. As he walks down the long hallway to Mr. Remington's office suites, Aaron nervously walks past the office of Kimberly Downing, Chief Financial Officer of the Remington Corporation and greets her.

"Good morning Kimberly. Mr. Remington called me down for a meeting," he says smiling at her. Without making eye contact with Aaron, Kimberly responds in a subtle voice.

"I know," she says continuing to type on her computer. As Aaron proceeds to Mr. Remington's office suite he is greeted and offered a seat.

"Well Aaron, how are you doing this morning? Come on in and have a seat" says Remington. As Aaron takes a seat he stares at Remington.

"I'm doing well, Is there a problem sir?" asks Aaron.

"No Aaron, I called you to my office to share some great news I received this morning about you. I received a call from the Awards Recognition Committee of the Fortune 500 Foundation. They called to inform me that the Remington Corporation was selected as one of the top Fortune 500 companies this year. As you're aware the Fortune 500 Foundation award is one of the most prestigious awards a company can receive. I also found out that the two contracts you successfully bided on with Cardinal Enterprises and SAS Systems got us on the Fortune 500 Foundation listing. Thank to your leadership and the fact that your bids awarded us with over fifty three million dollars on those contracts is why we made the list. In all my years running this corporation this has been a dream come true," says Remington. As Mr. Remington stands up from his chair and walks over to Aaron and embraces him he hands Aaron a white envelope. Opening it Aaron realizes there is a check inside it in the amount of fifty thousand dollars made out to him from the Remington Corporation. As Aaron smiles in excitement Mr. Remington responds.

"Thank you Aaron for the outstanding job you have done since joining us here at the Remington Corporation. Because you have worked tirelessly day and night securing those bids and because of the national attention we've received I wanted to show you my love and appreciation in financial gratitude.

"Thank you Mr. Remington for this bonus! This is the best gift I have ever received in my life," says Aaron. After embracing Mr. Remington, Aaron leaves the office smiling as he walks past Kimberly who again doesn't speak or acknowledge him as he exits and goes back to his office. As he arrives back to his office Aaron immediately picks up his cell phone off his desk and calls his wife to tell her the great news. After several rings his wife answers the phone.

"Hello Aaron, what's wrong?" says Asia realizing he just left home an hour ago. Curious to why Aaron is calling her this early in the morning she seems worried.

"Is everything okay?" she asks. Aaron replies in excitement.

"Hey baby, I have some great news to share with you. You're not going to believe this Asia!" says Aaron. Asia pauses awaiting the exciting news.

"This morning Mr. Remington called me into his office. I was thinking it had something to do with a missed assignment or a mistake I made when it came to the bidding process. You know, most times when you're called into your boss's office this early in the morning it's usually for something you did wrong. Well, Mr. Remington called me into his office to inform me that the Remington Corporation is the recipient of this year's Fortune 500 Foundation Award as one of the top financial corporations in the country," says Aaron. Aaron then takes a brief pause to gather himself emotionally before speaking back to his wife.

"Hold on! Hold on baby! That's not all! Mr. Remington told me that the reason why we was on the list is because of my ability of securing several bids. It was the ones that I bid on with Cardinal Enterprise and SAS Systems. Then after congratulating me he reached inside his suit-coat pocket and pulled out an envelope. Baby, in that envelope was a check made out to me from the Remington Corporation for fifty thousand dollars! Then, right before I called you, Mr. Remington he sent a voice message to my office phone inviting you and I to join him and his wife to the upcoming Fortune 500 Foundation awards dinner and ceremony in New York City next weekend. Can you believe that?" says Aaron. Hearing the great news Asia screams with joy through the phone and becomes very excited.

"Baby, that is awesome! I love you! I love you! I can't wait for you get home so I can give you a big hug and kiss!" she says. Attempting to regain his composure on the phone Aaron responds.

"Asia, the other reason I'm calling you is to tell you that we need to celebrate this special occasion. Let me show you my love by taking you to your favorite French Restaurant at Harbor Point. I want you to get dressed this evening in that sexy red satin dress that you know turns me on. I want you to let your hair down tonight so every man that see you will take a second look. I promise I won't get jealous again like I did last time," says Aaron. Hearing Aaron's comments Asia laughs out loud and replies.

"Aaron are you sure you'll be able to handle it when these men start looking at me? Do you know the last time I walked into that restaurant in that red mini and matching stiletto heels? I remember the last time that I wore that dress you got so jealous when the men were getting romantically paralyzed seeing me in that dress, even though most were with their dates. You know, I have gained a few more pounds on my backside since then so that red mini will be fitting me more tightly around the hips," says Asia laughing out loud. Hearing Asia speak, Aaron responds confidently.

"Baby, with all the money we got now, I will be okay now. As long as they look but don't P touch. I will be home at six o'clock sharp to surprise you," says Aaron. Asia is curious to what her husband meant by surprising her responds.

"Aaron, yes surprise me. I can't wait to see what the surprise will be this is evening. What are you planning on wearing this evening on our date? Or would you like me to pick something from out of your closet for you to wear?" asks Asia.

"Baby, I got it all covered. Let me surprise you this evening with my fashionable attire. Trust me, I will dress to impress, just for you! I will see my beautiful Queen at six o'clock sharp," says Aaron. Asia responds in her most soft gentle voice romantically.

"Okay I'll be ready when you get here baby. I love you!" she says as she ends the call. As Aaron prepares himself to get ready for an evening of romanticism, he immediately dials 411.

After three rings a young lady answers the phone.

"Hello directory assistance may I help you?" she says.

"Can you give me the number to Prichard Limousine Services," says Aaron. Hearing Aaron's request the operator responds.

"Just a moment please," she says. After a brief wait the operator returns to speak with Aaron.

"Sir, the telephone number is 305-222-0000. Would you like me to connect you?" asks the operator.

"Yes please," says Aaron. As she connects Aaron she responds pleasantly.

"Thank you for choosing directory assistance," she says as she connects Aaron. After several rings the reservation specialist from Prichard Limousine Services answers.

"Good Afternoon Prichard Limousine Services, may I help you?" asks the reservationist.

"Yes, name is Aaron Williams and I would like to make a reservation for one of your luxury stretch limousines for this evening," he says excitedly. After hearing Aaron's request for a luxury limousine the reservation specialist ask Aaron several questions regarding his reservation request.

"Sir, how many will be in your company this evening for our limousine?" she asks.

"Just me and my lovely wife," says Aaron. The Reservation Specialist looks over her list of available limousines on her computer and responds.

"Well sir, based on the number in your party it sounds like you need our smallest limousine that seats four. Would that be okay?" she asks.

Hearing the reservationist's availability and recommendations Aaron responds.

"Sorry, but this is a special occasion so I will need one of your larger luxury limousines you have available for this evening. You know like a Fortune 500 style limousine," says Aaron.

Not understanding what Aaron meant by a Fortune 500 style limousine the reservationist responds.

"We don't have a Fortune 500 style limousine; however, we have one of our top of the line stretch limousines. It seats twelve comfortably complete with a wet bar and a surround sound stereo system. The rate will be five hundred dollars an hour with a minimum of three hours. That does not include gratuity. This vehicle is usually reserved for celebrities, corporate leaders and does dignitaries," says the reservationist. After hearing the rates and the type of people the reservationist mentioned of who reserves those limousines, Aaron responds positively.

"Consider me a corporate executive dignitary and I want to reserve that luxury limousine," says Aaron. Going into the computer screen again she brings up the luxury limousine and began to ask Aaron a series of questions to confirm his reservation.

"How are you willing to pay for this rental? We only accept credit card or corporate accounts?" says the reservationist.

"I will be paying with my American Express. My card number is 1471209982131156 with an expiration date of May 2025 and my three-digit number on the back is 122," says Aaron. After processing Aaron's card and seeing it was approved the reservationist responds.

"Mr. Williams where would you like to have our chauffeur pick you up?" she asks. Aaron pulls out his itinerary for the evening written on a piece of paper from his suit coat.

"The first pickup will be at the Pyramid Office Towers located at 224 Corporate Boulevard at 5:30 p.m. Then we will pick up at 35408 Cherry Blossom Lane to pick up my beautiful wife. From thee we will go to the Harbor Pointe Revolving Restaurant on the beach. After dinner and drinks we will end our night at the Regency Hotel downtown where the chauffeur will take us where we will stay for the night. I have one other request. If you could have in the limousine a dozen white roses, a bottle of Regal Chablis wine, you know the one that is imported from France on ice with two heart shape wine glasses along with some soft romantic music on your surround sound system," says Aaron. As the reservationist types in the information into her computer she responds.

"I have all the amenities that you requested and our Chauffeur will have your luxury limousine at your first pickup on time Mr. Williams. Anything else I can assist you with today?" she asks.

"I think that we will be all that we will need," says Aaron.

"Mr. Williams thanks for choosing Prichard Limousine Service and have a wonderful day," says the receptionist. After ending his call with Prichard Limousine Services, Aaron understanding that he has a short amount of time for preparation turns out the lights to his office before closing the door. As he approaches the receptionist desk he smiles at Camille before saying goodbye for the day.

"Camille, I'm leaving for the rest of the day. If anyone needs to reach me I am available by cell phone. I'm leaving early to spend some time with my beautiful wife by taking her on a dining experience she will never forget. Have a great weekend," says Aaron. Camille smiles back and poses a question for Aaron.

"Aaron, one day I was hoping that you can sit down with my husband and talk to him about the importance of taking his beautiful wife out and spending some quality time with her as well?" says Camille. Aaron looks at Camille surprised at her request before responding.

"Camille, why don't you do the complete opposite and surprise him by taking him out to dinner. That will make him think twice to what he as a husband should do for his beautiful wife. I will assure you it will not be a problem anymore," says Aaron smiling. Camille stares at Aaron in disbelief to how simple he made her issue so resolvable. Before leaving the office he looks back at Camille and smiles at her and speaks.

"Camille, I'm not trying to be flirtatious but you're such a beautiful lady and so is my wife. If you do what I suggested I think your husband will feel guilty and he probably will be taking you out to dinner every week," says Aaron. As Aaron smiles at Camille, he leaving the office and hurriedly makes his way to the elevator to descend to the ground floor. As Aaron walks to the elevator to the parking garage and gets in his car, he drops the top of his shiny black Mercedes sports car. He takes the Airport Boulevard exit then turns left into the parking lot and turns into the parking lot of Vito's Italian Men's Wear. Exiting his car, Aaron walks into the clothing store to be fitted for a designer suit to wear for the evening. There he is greeted by the owner and tailor Vito.

"Hello sir, my name is Vito. How I can help you today?" says Vito.

"I am looking for a white designer double breasted suit to wear for this evening," says Aaron. As Vito looks at Aaron's physique he responds.

"Let me guess, you're a 32 in length, 38 waist size," says Vito. Hearing Vito speak with an Italian accent Aaron was shocked to see how accurate he was in the guessing of his clothing measurements.

"You're are right on the money with my measurements. You're an expert," says Aaron.

Vito smiles at Aaron before responding back.

"I'm Italian, right brother? And Italians are known for knowing about two things, the finest in men's suits and how to treat beautiful women. That's why I own the finest men's wear store in town," says Vito. Vito directs Aaron to follow him down the aisle where there is racks of suits on display. As he takes a double breasted white suit off the rack, he hands it to Aaron. Aaron holds up the suit next to him and smiles, then looks at Vito.

"Bingo my brother! This suit is perfect for you, size 38 waist and 32 length with the coat size of 42. You came to the right store. You got a good taste for classy suits. You appear to be a playboy my brother. Seem like you getting ready to pick up a sexy lady for the evening?" says Vito. Hearing Vito's comments Aaron smiles.

"As a matter of fact I am, but that sexy beautiful lady just happens to be my wife," says Aaron.

Vito looks at Aaron smiling back.

"I'm sorry my brother, no disrespect to you or your wife. I just figured that you wearing threads like this means that you're going to be in the company of a beautiful lady. In your case, it happens to be your wife," says Vito. With the suit in hand, Vito directs Aaron over to the dressing room to be fitted.

"Why don't you go in the dressing room and try it on to make sure everything fits. By the way, the last person who came in and bought a suit like this from me was a former NFL star player who went by the name Neon Deion. You heard of him right? He was the star athlete that told the NFL team that wanted to draft him out of college that in order for them to sign him to a contract for the money he wanted that they would have to put him in layaway," says Vito. Vito laughs out loud as Aaron goes into the dressing room to be fitted into the suit. Moments later, Aaron comes out of the dressing room wearing the designer suit smiling.

"It's almost like the designer who tailored this suit made it just for me. I want to wear it out of the store. I just took the corporation I work for to Fortune 500 status by securing two bids worth over fifty three million dollars. In fact, my wife and I am going to New York City next weekend to receive the award with the President and CEO of the corporation. This evening I'm taking my beautiful wife out this evening for a celebration dinner and whatever comes next romantically if you know what I mean?" says Aaron.

"That's awesome my brother! You mean someone in Corporate America is giving credit to a black man for taking their company to Fortune 500 status? Excuse me my brother, I hope you don't take this as a negative, but I'm an Italian brother and nobody has given me credit for shit for what I've done for them. I have suited some of the most famous celebrities in this country putting them in some of the finest Italian designer suits and accessories. I have dressed men who were on Wall Street, who have received national awards at the Grammys, Emmys and well-known events. I have dressed Presidents my brother, even your first black President," says Vito. Vito gets noticeably angry talking about his experiences and speaks out loudly.

"I want my reparations too dammit!" says Vito turning his anger into a smile, Aaron smiles as he looks in the mirror.

"I hear you brother. It just happens that I got an owner of a different color who is very appreciative of my ability to make him some money," says Aaron.

"Tell you what my brother, when you get back to wherever you work do me a big favor? Get with the owner and put him on ice and frame his ass. Why? Because you probably won't find another owner like him in Corporate America. By the way, how does the suit feel on you?" says Vito. Aaron models the suit in front of Vito.

"It fits perfectly. So perfect, that I'm going to go back to my office and wear it out of the store. Do you have a garment bag to put my clothes in?" says Aaron.

"Sure, I'll be right back," says Vito. As Vito goes behind the counter to retrieve a garment bag, he hands it to Aaron to put his clothes in. Aaron gives Vito his credit card to pay for the purchase. As Vito goes to the register to ring up the purchase, he looks back at Aaron and makes a suggestion.

"My brother, I think you need some fashionable accessories to bring that suit out you boiught. I recommend that you get a white silk shirt and lay a red silk tie on it with a red handkerchief to put in your suit coat. I also suggest you wear a pair of my cherry red kicks that happens to be on sale. They are the perfect shoes for that suit," says Vito. As Vito directs Aaron over to the shoes, Aaron tries them on and likes their fit. He then picks up a shirt, tie and handkerchief and goes to the register to purchase them. Vito looks at Aaron smiling.

"Brother, if I would've let you get out of here with only that suit you been in trouble. Now you're going to be the fashion talk of the town tonight with your beautiful wife on your arm. Have a great romantic evening my brother," says Vito. With his suit on and accessories in his garment bag, Aaron thanks Vito as he walks out of the store. Getting in his is car, Aaron speeds off down the freeway back to the Pyramid Office Towers to his office as he waits for the arrival of the limousine. As he looks at his watch Aaron notices that it is already five o'clock as he walks from his car into the building. Walking into his office, Aaron takes out his cell phone to check on his wife before freshening up and grooming his hair to look very handsome for his wife when he arrives to pick her up in the limo. Making sure everything he is wearing is fitting perfectly, Aaron looks out of the window and notices that the white stretch limo has arrived. As Aaron takes the elevator to the lobby and walks out the doors of the Pyramid Office Towers, he greets the Chauffeur and introduces himself.

"Hello, I'm Aaron Williams. I'm ready to go pick up my Queen," says Aaron.

"Yes sir," says Aaron. As the Chauffeur smiles and graciously opens the door for Aaron he looks at his travel schedule on his limousine computer tablet for his next destination. As Aaron looks over the interior of the limousine he notices that he has all the amenities he had requested. As the limousine slowly takes off in route to the freeway, Aaron smiles in anticipation to their arrival to pick up his wife Asia. Arriving at his beautiful home on Cherry Blossom Lane the stretch limousine slowly pulls up near the driveway. As the Chauffeur comes to a complete stop Aaron takes out his cell phone and calls his wife notifying her that her King has arrived.

"Hey baby, your King has arrived to pick up his beautiful Queen," says Aaron. As the Chauffeur gets out of the limo awaiting Asia's arrival, Aaron smiles in anticipation of her presence. Moments later Asia comes out of the house looking glamorous like a celebrity model. Wearing a cherry red satin mini dress that exposes her sexy chocolate tone legs, Asia slowly walks towards the limousine. Her dress has a plunging neckline revealing her cleavage and the outline of her firm breast. She compliments her evening wear with a pair of black diamond teardrop earrings, a diamond studded necklace that sits perfectly between her breast, off black designer stocking, a cherry red clutch purse and red stilettos. Draped over her shoulders is a black silk cape that enhances her elegant look. As she walks closer to the limousine, she falls into the waiting arms of her husband. Her silky black shoulder length hair is glistening in the sun as it bounces in place with her every move. Aaron smiles as he embraces his wife, giving her a passionate kiss before helping her into the limousine. When the chauffeur closes the door the feel of passion and romantic love takes over. As the chauffeur slowly drives out to the main thoroughfare, Aaron and Asia starts cozying up to each other. The chauffeur at the request of Aaron turns up the music to a moderate level in the rear of the limo. As the music plays romantic music as they travel smoothly down the freeway, Aaron reaches on the shelf of the wet bar and grabs the bottle of Regal Chablis. Getting two glasses and a thong to place the ice in the glasses, he slowly pours Asia and him a drink. As he hands Asia her glass they give each other a toast to their success.

"To my lovely wife, may we continue enjoy our happy marriage and achieve financial success for as long as we live, cheers!" says Aaron. Aaron gives Asia a passionate kiss before taking a drink. As Asia looks around the limo she notices rose petals scattered indicating Aaron's romantic affection for her. She smiles romantically at Aaron and responds.

"The last time you and I had rose petals in our presence was the night we made passionate love to each other after we got married,' says Asia. As the limousine arrives to the entrance of the Harbor Pointe Revolving Restaurant one of the finest five star restaurants in Chapel, the chauffeur opens the door and assist Asia out. As Aaron and Asia walks toward the entrance of the restaurant they are immediately greeted by the Concierge who welcomes them to the Harbor Pointe Revolving Restaurant.

"Hello Monsieur and Madame. Under what name are we holding your reservations this evening?" he asks.

"The reservations are under the name Aaron Williams," says Aaron. Looking over the reservation list on his computer tablet the Concierge acknowledges the couple's reservation and escorts them to an open elevator taking them to the revolving restaurant on the twelfth floor. As the elevator ascends to the floor, Aaron and Asia is graciously greeted by the restaurant's Maître D, who is informed by the Concierge the name of the guests. Walking up to Aaron and Asia the Maître D makes his formal greeting.

"Hello Monsieur and Madame, welcome to the Harbor Pointe Revolving Restaurant. Follow me to your seats please," he says. Following the Maître D to their table both Aaron and Asia are extremely impressed with the romantic and soft atmosphere of the five-star restaurant. Arriving to their table located in a very romantic dimly lit area the Maître D seats Asia.

"Your waiter Pierre will be here to serve you shortly. Enjoy your dining experience," he says.

While waiting for the waiter to arrive Aaron reaches inside his suit coat pocket and pulls out the envelope containing the fifty thousand dollar check and hands it to his wife.

"This is for you baby. It's for you believing in me through all that we have been through. Without you none of this could have been achieved," says Aaron. Aaron takes Asia's hand romantically. As tears start to trickle down from her eyes, Asia is emotionally filled with joy as she looks at her husband.

"Aaron, I love you! It is an honor being married to you," she says looking at him romantically. Moments later the waiter comes to the table and greets the couple.

"Hello Madame and Monsieur, my name is Pierre and I will be your waiter for the evening. Like to start off with something to drink?" he asks. Aaron takes a brief look at the wine menu then looks at the waiter.

"Yes, we will like to have a bottle of your Regal Chablis on ice with two heart shaped glasses," hesays. The waiter smiles at the couple as he writes down their order.

"I will be right back with your Regal Chablis, he says. As the waiter begins to leave the table Aaron interrupts him and curiously asks.

"Did you forget something? I think something is missing?' says Aaron staring at him in curiosity. The waiter remembering what Aaron was alluding to gives Aaron a smile and nod of understanding.

"I got it Monsieur," he says. Reaching over and taking his wife's hand, Aaron whispers romantically.

"I love you. Soon we are going to be so financially successful that anything you want won't be a problem," says Aaron. Moments later the waiter brings a bouquet of red and white roses and hands them to Asia and leaves the table. Shocked at the presence of the roses, Asia gets very emotional as she shakes while holding the bouquet. Realizing that she is becoming unstable holding her gift, Aaron takes them and places them in the chair across from him as they prepare to dine. Then Aaron opens a small jewelry box and pulls out an eighteen-karat diamond studded ring and places it gently on his wife's finger next to her wedding ring.

"This is to show of my devotion and love for you Asia. I hope that you will cherish this moment for the rest of your life," says Aaron. As tears begin to stream down Asia's face, she becomes speechless through it all. She gives her husband a lengthy romantic kiss ignoring the fact that other restaurant guests nearby are watching them. As the waiter arrives at the table ready to take their order, Aaron smiles at him thanking him for assisting in celebrating his wife's engagement.

"Madame and Monsieur, may I get you an appetizer to start you off?" asked the waiter. Aaron looks over the menu then looks at his wife.

"Do you want some appetizers? Ask Aaron. Asia responds immediately.

"No honey you already know what I want as an entrée," says Asia. Hearing Asia's response Aaron responds to the waiter.

"I think we will pass on the appetizers and we will have the prime rib dinner with scallop potatoes, asparagus dipped in cream sauce and honey carrots," says Aaron. As the waiter leaves the table, Aaron leans back in his chair and romantically says to Asia.

"We're not going home baby, I've made reservations for us to have a romantic night at the Regency Hotel downtown, "says Aaron smiling at Asia. Asia smiles back and responds.

"The way you're making me feel this evening is so romantic. I promise baby, I won't disappoint you intimately when we get to the Regency Hotel tonight," says Asia giving Aaron a lustful kiss. As the waiter brings their entrée to the table, Aaron prepares a space making sure there is room to place their meals. As the waiter leaves, Aaron and Asia casually enjoy their meal under candlelight. After dinner Aaron and Asia leaves the restaurant to their waiting limousine as the chauffeur opens the door to take them to the Regency Hotel for a night of relaxation and yes, intimacy.

Chapter 2

Sitting on a park bench drinking a bottle of wine is Robert Remington Jr., the son of the President/CEO of the Remington Corporation's Robert Remington Sr. He is a conversation with his friend David, who is also an alcoholic. Looking physically disheveled, Rob is arguing with David over who needs to buy the next bottle of wine. As their conversation continues to get escalated, David changes the subject to Rob's family.

"Rob, I wish I was in your shoes. With all the money your father has and promised you the company after he retires. How could you screw that up by becoming a drunk?" says David. Turning red and getting very upset, Rob stares at David after taking another drink of wine from his bottle.

"Shut the hell up! You have no idea what I went through. He promised me that damn company after I graduated from college but he wanted me to kiss his ass, begging him for money while he treated me like a dog. He was always on me about who I associated with and my lifestyle. Then he turn around and hire this black guy as his Vice President of Operations. And you ask me why I'm a damn alcoholic? I hate the hell out of him!" says Rob Jr. David shakes his head in shame as he stares at Rob.

"You had it made Rob," says David. Rob Jr. looks at David angrily and shouts at him.

"What in the hell do you mean?" says Rob Jr. David again stares at Rob surprised that he doesn't understand.

"What I mean is getting in the condition that you're in today. You could have easily been on top of the world man!" says David. Rob again looks at David in dismay and again shouts at him.

"I think that's a bunch of shit! He always wanted others to think that he loved me but he really hated me the day that I was born. If it wasn't for my mom I would probably have been dead!" say Rob Jr. David looks at Rob and shakes his head.

"Man, I can hear your eulogy now, Robert Remington Jr. loving son of Sarah and Robert Remington Sr., President and CEO of the Remington Corporation who died homeless from complications of a poor relationship with his daddy, depression, and being a drunk and what he thought was reverse discrimination by his daddy. Rob, why don't you get yourself sober, check into a rehab center and show your dad that you're ready to take over the company when he retires since he promised it to you," says David. Moments later David observes Rob's older sister coming up the walkway into the park. Spotting her brother sitting on the bench Deena walks closely towards him smiling.

"I figured I would find you here Rob," says Deena staring at him. Rob Jr. looks over at his sister and starts to get very frustrated by her presence.

"What the hell do you want?" says Rob Jr. angrily. Deena takes a seat on the park bench next to her brother in hopes of bringing him some good family news.

"Rob, I came here to tell you that dad's company made this year's Fortune 500 list as one of the top businesses in the country. Mom asks me to try to find you and invite you to the house for a celebration dinner at six o'clock in dad's honor this evening before they leave for New York City to attend the awards presentation this weekend," says Deena. Rob stares at Deena giving her an inquisitive look.

"So I guess I'm supposed to be delighted and humble myself to that bastard huh? Yeah I know how it goes. I come over to dinner to hear everything he has done for the company and the family only to get ridiculed by him," says Rob Jr. Deena, listening to Rob's verbal tirade of her dad responds angrily.

"Don't blame mom or dad for your problems. They gave you everything you needed to succeed in life. They sent you to one of the best schools in the country, Harvard University where you got your master's degree. Rob, you chose your own path of destruction. If you were smart you would get yourself in an alcohol rehab program to deal with your alcoholism. After getting yourself clean maybe you can start talking to dad about giving you another chance to run his company. Rob, why did you waste your time going to college only to end up on the streets being a drunk?" says Deena. Rob, after hearing his sister berate him shouts out to her in response to her comments.

"Oh blame me! Blame me for everything that went wrong in our family and in my life Deena, How soon have you forgotten the times when dad used to come home from work drunk and beat the hell out of us for nothing? I guess that was my fault too huh? I guess it was my fault for him being an alcoholic as well? Now you wonder why I'm like I am, a drunk! Since dad's company is a Fortune 500 company I guess all those things should be forgotten huh? Well Deena it's not. Dad is a lying, abusive and cheating no good... Deena, tired of Rob's verbal assault on her dad, interrupts his conversation.

"I don't have to sit here and listen to you discredit our family. It's about you Rob! You need to clean up your life before you start dirtying up others. I thought I would also let you know that mom went to the doctor on Wednesday and she found out that she has breast cancer. She has to go in for a biopsy and additional test in the next few weeks. Rob, you need to get yourself together, put your feelings aside and be there for mom. The family celebration starts at 7:00 p.m. Friday and mom wants you to be there," says Deena as she angrily. Deena, with a serious look on her face and obviously upset, gets up from the park bench and walks away without saying goodbye. Rob, in a moment of sadness hearing of his mom being diagnosed with breast cancer places his face in the palm of his hands hiding the tears that are streaming down his face. Realizing Rob's emotional pain in finding out his mom's illness, David stays silent out of respect of what he is going through. Rob Jr. gets up from the bench without saying a word or acknowledging

David walks away stumbling through the park obviously intoxicated. Concerned about Rob's safety, David gets up and follows Rob in hope of providing support through his most difficult times. As he gets closer to Rob, David shouts out loudly.

"Rob! Rob! Let me talk to you! I know you're upset," says David. Rob slowly turns around stumbling and looks at David as tears continue to stream down his face.

"David, shut the hell up! You have no idea what I'm going through. Leave me the hell alone!" he says. Rob Jr. continues to walk stumbling across the street almost getting hit by a vehicle as he goes into the neighborhood halfway house where he is residing. As Sarah is setting up the dining table in preparation for the celebration dinner for the Remington Corporation, Deena walks in the room with a sad look on her face. Concerned as to why her daughter is looking sad, Sarah inquiries about what is going on.

"What's going on Deena? What's wrong?" asks Sarah. Deena looks at her mom and speaking clearly.

"I saw Rob today at the park and I told him about dad's company making the Fortune 500 list and the celebration dinner that was being held in his honor this evening. Unfortunately, he was not impressed. Rob is still blaming dad for everything that has went wrong in his life. Mom, he's not taking any responsibility for what's he has done personally that has caused his problems. Not surprised at what Deena is sharing, Sarah stares at Deena.

"Did Rob say he was coming over for dinner this evening?" asks Sarah. Deena looks at her mom and shakes her head solemnly.

"No he didn't but in the condition that he was in I don't think so. The way he was talking about dad and blaming him for all his problems I doubt it. I think it would take a miracle for him to show up this evening," says Deena. Sarah shakes her head in disappointment.

"It's a shame that Rob still feels that way Deena. We tried to give him everything he needed. I don't understand his bitterness toward his dad," says Sarah. As their conversation continues, Sarah interrupts her daughter's conversation to get back in the kitchen to prepare the celebration dinner realizing that her husband will be home soon. Realizing her mom's urgency to get everything prepared Deena looks at mom and smiles.

"Go ahead mom and get things together. I need to go home and get dressed. I will see you soon," says Deena as she walks out the door to her car. About an hour later Sarah's husband Robert comes home appearing to be in a joyful mood. After greeting Robert with a hug and a kiss Sarah encourages her husband to go and freshen up in preparation for the celebration dinner. An hour later guests start arriving for the dinner celebration. As Deena greets them at the door and walks them into the spacious and elegant dining room to be seated. As all the invited guest are seated, and dinner is placed on the table Robert Remington Sr. takes the time to greet everyone and prepares to open up the festivity with a prayer. As the time reaches six o'clock and everything is prepared for the special dinner celebration, Robert Remington Sr. takes his seat at the head of the table, he greets his guest.

"Greetings and good evening. I want to personally thank all of you for joining me and my family for this dinner celebration. With that said, I would like to start us off with a prayer," says Robert Sr. Remington starts the prayer a loud knock comes to the door. Before he can start the prayer a loud knock comes to the door. Obviously upset that he has to stop the beginning of his prayer, Robert Remington stares at Deena who immediately gets up from the table to see who is at the door.

"Who is it?" asks Deena.

"It's Rob!" he says. Surprised to see that Rob showed up at the dinner celebration, Deena smiles as she greets him.

"Hello Rob, come on in! We've been waiting for you, "said Deena Giving him a hug, Deena walks Rob Jr. walks into the dining room as Sarah offers her son a seat as he greets the guest who are in attendance. Sarah, surprised to see her son in attendance gets up from her seat and gives him a warm embrace and kiss. Robert Sr., visibly upset see his son in attendance shakes his head.

"Hello, sorry I'm late," says Rob Jr. Disturbed by his son's presence and interruption of his prayer Remington sarcastically speaks up.

"May I try to start prayer again? Dear Heavenly Father we come to you this evening asking that you bless us as we celebrate my company's success in the business world, and it's recognition as a Fortune 500 Company. As my wife and I along with my Vice President of Operations and his wife prepare for our trip to New York City tomorrow for the awards ceremony, I ask that you make our trip a safe one for all involved. Last but not least Father, I ask that you allow individuals to get their lives in order so that they may not bring down the family name. I ask these and all things in your son Jesus name Amen. You may go ahead and eat," says Remington. As Deena sneaks a look at her mom realizing that her dad purposely directed the end of the prayer toward Rob and his lifestyle as well as his problems with alcohol. As the family and guests start preparing their plates, passing food dishes around to each other Remington stares at Rob in disgust. Sarah, realizing the negative vibes generated by her husband toward her son attempts to initiate some positive intervention.

"Junior, it's so good to see you! How have you been son?" asks Sarah. Rob looks at his mom smiling.

"I've been surviving," says Rob. As he prepares his plate his dad speaks out from across the table.

"You decided to come out of the cold huh, Rob?" says Remington Sr. Sarah again intervenes before Rob Jr. could respond.

"Honey, please eat your food," pleads Sarah. Looking at his wife Remington Sr. replies.

"I was just welcoming him back home," says Remington Sr. sarcastically. As Sarah attempts be respectful, considering that they have family and guests in their presence Sarah again responds.

"All l I'm saying dear is let's talk after dinner" she says. Seeing that his dad wants to create problems with him, Rob Jr. interrupts his mother.

"Mom, let him talk. Dad, do you have something to say to me?" says Rob speaking clearly while staring at him and staring at him awaiting a response. Robert Sr. stares back at Rob in anger.

"Hell yes, I have something to say. In fact I have a lot to say. It's a shame that you have tarnished the image of this family by turning into a drunk. I had you all set up to take over the company after I retired. I sent you to a prestigious college, Harvard University to get your business degree and what did you do? Wasted all my damn money and destroyed my dreams. Look at you, you are a damn bum!" says Remington Sr. Rob, allowing his dad to go through his verbal tirade calmly gets up out of his seat pushing his plate away from him, causing tension among the family and guests. Rob, staring at his dad raises his voice across the table.

"Yeah, you sent me to college to get my degree. You did all that for your own self-image. I destroyed your dreams huh? What about the dreams you destroyed, when you use to come home from work drunk and were physically abusive to Deena and me? Remember when you threatened that you would kill us if we told mom of your physical abuse? You talk about destroying your dreams. What about the way you destroyed mom's dreams, when she found out about Rodney? You know Rodney, the child you had outside your marriage that you hid from mom by paying child support under the table to keep it quiet. That arrangement worked until little Rodney became a teenager and tried to extort money from you. Realizing that he was going to go public, then, and only then was when you confessed your sins to your wife. What a poor example of a father. All the while you were giving your colleagues and friends the impression that you were in a so-called happy marriage. You are nothing but a good for nothing-old ass infidel. Yeah I'm telling all of your business, or as you would call it letting the skeletons out of the closet. Now I'm asking you, is that a dream or a reality," Rob says angrily staring at his dad and mom. Hearing what his son has shared and the embarrassment among his guest, Robert Sr. gets up out of his chair in a fury, walks over toward Rob and confronts him.

"Don't you ever talk to me like that!" he says. Without any hesitation Robert Sr. slaps Rob in the face.

"Get the hell out of my house you no good bum!" Robert Sr. screams. As Rob takes a step back from the effect of his dad's physical assault, he walks toward the door. Looking back at his dad he angrily replies.

"Yeah dad, the truth hurts don't it, Mr. Fortune 500? I hope your colleagues and friends don't find out about the real Robert Remington Sr. and the devil hiding behind his successful company, dressed in his blue Brooks Brothers suits," says Rob Jr. As Rob Jr. leaves slamming the door behind him, the family and guest are in a state of shock of what they had just heard and their reaction to it. As Mr. Remington goes back to his seat, he apologizes to his guests for the outburst between him and his son. He then asked everyone to stay seated and continue to enjoy the meal that his wife so gracefully has prepared.

Chapter 3

Arriving at the Miami International Airport, Aaron and Asia are carrying their carry-on baggage to Concourse A where they are scheduled to meet the Remington's for their scheduled 10:45 A.M. flight to New York City. Arriving at the airport concourse, Aaron spots Mr. Remington and his wife at the will call section of the ticket window. Directing his wife Asia to follow him, Aaron walks up near the line.

"Good Morning Mr. and Mrs. Remington!" says Aaron. Turning around and seeing Aaron and his wife, Mr. Remington smiles.

"Well Good Morning Aaron and Asia. Are you ready to enjoy the most fabulous event in the country?" says Mr. Remington. Aaron smiles at Mr. Remington radiantly.

"We are most honored to accompany you and your wife to this event," he says glowingly.

Getting their tickets and checking in their luggage, Mr. Remington urges his wife along with Aaron and Asia to follow him to the Concourse security checkpoint. After going through a thorough search by airport security, the couples are allowed to enter the tunnel leading to the entrance of their commercial flight. As they settle into their seats as the turbo engines revved up preparing for takeoff to their destination, New York City. Upon take off, the stewardess walks pass passengers smiling making sure that they have their seat belts on. After a video recording regarding flight safety and a greeting from the pilot, commercial flight 4409 takes off. After two hours of non-stop flight, the plane circles and eventually lands at La Guardia International Airport making a loud noise as it eases it's speed leading up to the unloading ramp. Getting their carry on out of the luggage compartment above, Aaron and Asia along with Mr. Remington and his wife exits the plane. As the couples are walking through the Concourse, Asia looks at Sarah smiling.

"Sarah, don't we have two of the most awesome men in the world?" she asks

"Yes we do, but it took our feminine persuasion has helped them get to where they are," she says laughing out loud. Asia joins Sarah in their laughs as they take the escalator down to the baggage claims area. As Aaron and Robert Sr. identify and take their luggage off the baggage carousel they join their wives to board a taxi to the Hilton Hotel, host of the Fortune 500 event. As they enter the lavish and spacious Hilton Hotel, both couples approach the registration desk to check in for a weekend of fun and excitement. Once registration is completed the bellhop with luggage in tow smiles and politely escorts them to the open elevator to their prospective rooms. After arriving to their room, Aaron takes a sigh of relief as he looks out the bay window of his room then smiles at his wife.

"New York City, the city that doesn't sleep," says Aaron as he continues to view the skyline from the twelfth floor. Asia smiles as she goes over to the window to see the view and give her husband a kiss.

"Baby, you earned this experience and I'm so proud of you," says Asia. After a romantic evening of sightseeing through the streets of New York City, viewing landmarks, and listening to a gifted musician share his talents on the street corners and sidewalks, Aaron and Asia stop for dinner. Entering an Italian restaurant called D'Amico, Aaron and Asia are cordially seated in this casual but contemporary restaurant. Moments later the waitress comes to the table and introduces herself.

"Hello my name is Cindy and can I get you something to drink?" she asks. Aaron politely looks at his wife waiting for her to respond.

"Yes, I would like a glass of iced tea with lemon," says Asia. Aaron follows up with his request.

"I'll have the same as my wife," he says smiling at the waitress. As the waitress scribbles their order on her pad, she proceeds to tell them what the special is for the day before leaving the table to get their beverages. After enjoying a very delicious dinner in a very intimate dining atmosphere Aaron and Asia pay their bill and casually exit the restaurant. Checking out the various entertainment venues, Aaron and Asia head back to the hotel stopping to take pictures of the neon glowing establishments. Once at the hotel, they head to the elevator taking them to their floor for a relaxing and romantic evening with each other. At daybreak the telephone rings several times startling Aaron who was in a deep sleep, tired from his active day before. Reaching over to the nightstand to pick up the receiver Aaron answers the phone.

"Hello, this is Aaron Williams," he says.

"Good Morning Aaron. I was calling to invite you and your wife down to breakfast in the hotel restaurant," says Mr. Remington.

"We would be happy to join you. What time are you planning on being there?" he says.

"Great, we will meet you in the restaurant in an hour," says Remington. Before getting out of bed, Aaron reaches over and puts his arm around his wife's shoulder and smiles at her causing her to respond. .

"Aaron, this has been some whirlwind two weeks for you. First, you were credited for the Remington Corporation receiving their Fortune 500 Foundation award. Then you received bonus check from Mr. Remington and now the trip here to New York City to be part of Mr. Remington receiving one of the most prestigious awards in the country. We have been blessed," says Asia. As Aaron smiles at Asia he reaches over and gives her a kiss.

"Let's just make sure that we stay humble through it all because we know that none of this would be possible without God." says Aaron. Looking at the clock on the night stand Aaron looks at his wife.

"We better get up and get ready so we can be on time for breakfast," he says. After getting dressed, Aaron and Asia leave their hotel room and head towards the elevator down the hallway. After arriving in the hotel lobby they stop by the registration desk to get information about restaurant location. After receiving information about the location of Temple Restaurant where they're scheduled to meet the Remington's for breakfast. Entering the restaurant Aaron immediately spot. Robert and Sarah seated at table for four. Walking up to the reservation podium Aaron informs greeter that their company is already seated and points in the direction where they are seated. As Aaron and Asia are escorted to the table, Mr. Remington gets up from his seat to greet Aaron and Asia.

"Good Morning, please have a seat and join us," says Remington. As Aaron and Asia take a seat the waiter greets them.

"Good morning, my name is Richard. Can I start you off with something to drink?" he asks.

After ordering two cups of coffee, the waiter leaves the table. Moments later the waiter arrives at the table with Aaron and Asia's coffee.

"Are you ready to order?" asks the waiter. Mr. Remington responds immediately.

"Since everyone is here I think we are ready to order. My wife and I would like to have your steak and egg combo with a bowl of fresh strawberries, two slices of wheat bread and two large glasses of orange juice," says Remington.

"How would you like your eggs and steaks sir?" he asks.

"We would like our eggs sunny side up and our steaks medium well please," he says. After taking the Remington's order the waiter looks over at Aaron and Asia.

"What would you two like to order?" he asks. Asia looks up at the waiter after viewing the menu.

"I will have the steak and egg combo as well with a bowl of fresh pineapples, a large glass of cranberry juice and a cup of regular coffee," she says smiling at the waiter.

"How would you like your steak and eggs?" asked the waiter. Asia responds immediately. I would like to have my eggs scrambled light and my steak well done please," says Asia. The waiter then looks at Aaron.

"And what would you like to have sir?" he asks. Aaron smiles as he looks at his wife.

"I would like to have exactly what my beautiful wife has ordered," says Aaron smiling at her.

"Now, that is love and that was so easy for me," says the waiter laughing. Both Aaron Asia laughs as the waiter as he leaves the table to place their order. Asia looks at Sarah smiling and curious.

"I must ask Sarah, how was it that your husband knew exactly what you wanted for breakfast without him asking you?" she said laughing. Sarah laughs and smiles at Asia.

"If you were married for 46 years like we have been, he'd better know what I want for breakfast, says Sarah smiling at her husband and nudging him. Asia looks at Aaron sarcastically.

"I hope Aaron doesn't get to know me that well," says Asia laughing. Asia looks at Aaron smiling and plants a kiss on her husband's cheek. As the couples continue their conversation and humor, the waiter arrives at the table with their breakfast. After placing their meals on the table, the waiter asked if there was anything else he can get for them. They all responded no thank you as Aaron says a prayer. Aaron while dining starts a conversation.

"Mr. Remington how does it feel this morning knowing, that this evening you will be receiving one of the most prestigious business awards in the nation?" asks Aaron. Mr. Remington glances over at his wife before responding.

"Well, it's a great feeling knowing that the hard work of many has brought me success with my company. It starts with the best woman in the world who happens to be my wife. Then it continues with the best employee I have ever hired who happens to be you Aaron. So to totally answer your question it was a teamwork effort. Tonight there will be cameras and videos from television and radio stations all across the country. They will be talking about our success," he says.

After eating a delightful breakfast and going around touring Time Square Aaron and Asia after a couple of hours of sightseeing goes back to their hotel room to rest before the evening celebration and gala. As time elapses and several hours before the black tie event, Asia is in the vanity mirror combing her silky jet-black hair. She looks over at her husband.

"Baby, I am so excited! Just think, we will be in the presence of some of the most successful business owners in the country," says Asia. As Aaron, goes to the bathroom to shave, he responds jubilantly.

"It will be a great event sweetheart. I want you to look gorgeous with all the bright lights and cameras flickering. We will be like celebrities in Hollywood," says Aaron. Hearing her husband's comments Asia smiles as she continues to style her hair and put on her makeup.

"Baby, you don't have to worry about me looking beautiful and dressing fabulous. I will be dressed to kill tonight," says Asia. As Aaron comes out of the bathroom, Asia gives her husband a seductive and romantic smile.

Chapter 4

After two hours of prepping both Aaron and Asia leave their hotel room for the reception gala prior to the awards banquet. Aaron, wearing an Italian designer black tuxedo and matching shiny black leather shoes with a white ruffled shirt and black bow tie. Asia dressed in a jet-black satin designer evening gown with a slit on the right side showing her sexy figure. She compliments her gown with matching black high heels stilettos accompanied with diamond studded matching teardrop earrings and a black clutch purse. Entering the elevator Aaron and Asia descend to the ground floor and exits to the lobby. Holding hands, Aaron and Asia stroll pass the registration desk to the entrance of the ballroom. Checking in at the guest desk, they are then escorted to the ballroom for the reception for all the honorees, families and dignitaries to meet and socialize. After two hours of socializing and drinking Aaron and Asia are taken into the ballroom to their reserved seats where Mr. Remington and his wife greets them.

"Hello Aaron and Asia, please join us," say Mr. Remington. As invited guest and recipients begin to flow into the ballroom and take their seats, Winston Millhouse, President of the Fortune 500 Foundation comes to the podium to begin the program and welcome everyone in attendance.

"Good Evening Fortune 500 Foundation Honorees, dignitaries and guests. Welcome to the 34th Annual Fortune 500 Foundation Awards Ceremony. We want to get started by acknowledging our newest and first time honorees on the Fortune 500 Foundation listing. First up on the list is the Remington Corporation. The Remington Corporation is a major public relations and marketing firm located in Chapel, Florida that has earned over one hundred and thirty one hundred million dollars during the year 2022. The tremendous success of this company has placed them on the Fortune 500 Foundation list at 498. I'm happy to introduce to you the President and CEO of the Remington Corporation, Mr. Robert Remington Sr. Please welcome to stage Mr. Robert Remington Sr." says Millhouse. As Mr. Remington gets up from his seat and receives congratulatory hugs form his wife, Aaron and Asia. As Mr. Remington walks up to the podium to a thunderous applause from the audience, he acknowledges them by waving in appreciation. Steadying himself at the podium Mr. Remington SR. receives the award and addresses the audience.

"Hello, first I would like to thank the Fortune 500 Foundation for this most prestigious honor. As all of you are aware, no company or corporation can achieve a Fortune 500 status without a successful team. I say that because our inclusion to this exclusive group had a lot to do with my Senior Account Executive Mr. Aaron Williams who is the primary reason that we are here today. He was able to secure major contracts that took us over fifty six million dollars in bids for our corporation. At this time I would like to bring to the podium our company's hero, Mr. Aaron Williams. Can you give him a round of applause?" says Remington. Aaron smiles with joy as he gets up from his seat, receiving congratulatory hugs from his wife and Sarah before joining Mr. Remington at the podium. After giving Remington a hug, Aaron goes to the podium. As Aaron takes a sigh of relief to regain his composure from the excitement he speaks.

"Thank you for the acknowledgment you have given me this evening. First, I want to thank God for giving me the gift of salesmanship. I also want to thank the Fortune 500 Foundation for your efforts in identifying our company the Remington Corporation for our achievements. And just as importantly, I want to thank Mr. Robert Remington Sr. the President and CEO of the Remington Corporation for giving me the opportunity utilizing my skill set to secure the contracts needed for us to reach this milestone as a corporation. He hired me, believed in me, an African American executive when other companies refused to give me a chance. Because of that I will be forever grateful," says Aaron. As Aaron steps away from the podium and goes back to his table to another round of applause and the continuous flickering of lights from cameras in his face. After the banquet and awards presentation the Remington's and William's make their way through a sea of honorees, dignitaries and guests out into the lobby area where individuals were giving each other congratulatory and farewell wishes before leaving the hotel. As Aaron and Asia walks through the crowd attempting to get to the elevators they are met by a group of reporters from various media outlets surrounding Aaron wanting interviews. With the flashing of the cameras in Aaron's face he politely attempts to answer some of the reporter's questions.

"Mr. Williams how does it feel to be the first African American executive to work for the Remington Corporation and achieve the status that you have?" asked the Reporter.

"It feels great not only as an African American, but a person who has been through so much to get where I am. I am so blessed," he says. Moments later another Reporter asks Aaron a question.

"Mr. Williams, how are your co-workers going to handle all the attention that you are receiving after being championed for getting your company this national recognition and award?" he ask.
Aaron smiles at the reporter and replies candidly.

"I thought Mr. Remington made that very clear in his acceptance speech. Didn't you hear it?" asks Aaron. Knowing that it is getting late and his wife is getting weary from all of the day's activities, Aaron responds to the reporters.

"I will take one more question please," says Aaron.

"Amber Williams, I am a local reporter from Chapel covering this story where the Remington Corporation is located. I remember doing a story with Mr. Remington Sr. where he had said that his son, Robert

Jr. would be his successor when he retired. My question is in two parts. Where is Robert Jr.? And my second question is how that will affect your position in the corporation if what he said becomes a reality?" she asks. Catching Aaron off guard with such sensitive question, he replies nonchalantly.

"I think those are questions that you would have to ask Mr. Remington. I am not in a position to respond to that. Thanks for your questions. The wife is getting tired and we need to rest up for tomorrow," says Aaron. As Aaron and Asia walks away from the barrage of questions that reporters continue to ask him, Mr. Remington looks over at Aaron and smiles before getting into the elevator with his wife.

Chapter 5

Arriving at the Care Unit Treatment Center Rob realizes that his drinking has become so serious to the extent where he needed to be admitted into alcohol rehab facility. As he enters the facility and walks up to the information desk he is greeted by the Information Specialist.

"Good morning! May I help you?" asked the Information Specialist. Rob Jr, looking very stressed and irritated stares at the female specialist.

"I'm here to sign myself in to get dried out," says Rob Jr. Hearing Rob Jr. request, she inquires for more information.

"What is your name please?" ask the Specialist.

"My name is Robert Remington Jr. but not like my dad." he says. Shocked at Rob's response the specialist looks at her admissions sheet. Not seeing Rob's name on the list she looks up at Rob and replies.

"Sir, don't see you on the admissions list. Mr. Remington, were you referred here at the treatment center?" she asks. Rob stares at the Specialist, gets upset and raises his voice.

"No, didn't you hear me say what I said? I want to sign myself in to get dried out?" says Rob getting more upset. Putting the specialist on alarm by his behavior. She pushes her chair back making sure she has accessibility to the security radio if needed. The specialist calmly tries to explain the admission procedures.

"Sir, I'm sorry but you can only be admitted to the Care Unit if you were referred by your physician or treated into the emergency room to be admitted," she says. Rob Jr, listening to the Specialist comments about admission to the facility gets very upset. He immediately starts pacing the floor, then all of a sudden violently starts kicking furniture and knocking magazines off the table as he rants profanity. The Specialist realizes that Rob Jr.is close to getting physically aggressive picks up her radio and calls CU security.

"Security to CU main lobby, stat! Security to CU we have a male subject who is being very unruly and destroying property. Please come stat to the reception area. As the Specialist puts down her radio, she gives Rob his space in hopes that he calms down before security arrives. "Sir, I have someone coming down to assist you," says the Specialist. As the Specialist speak calmly to Rob Jr. he walks up on the specialist screaming.

"I don't want to see no damn person to come see me! I told you I need help!" says Rob.
Moments later three hospital security officers show up in the lobby observing Rob going into what they believe is an emotional meltdown. Cautiously approaching him the security officers surrounds him to avoid any continued aggressive behavior. Rob feeling crowded by the security officers screams at them.

"Either admit me or I'm going to kill myself!" he says. Hearing Rob's comments physical tirade and threats of suicide and his attempts to leave the area the security supervisor immediately ordered that Rob Jr.be physically restrained while a call was being made to the Chapel Police Department. Moments later the local police arrive at the scene. After a detail discussion of Rob's volatile behavior and the threat of suicide the life squad unit was called to transport him to University Hospital Psychiatric Emergency for treatment. Arriving at University Hospital Psychiatric Emergency, Rob Jr. is met by hospital security as the ambulance pulls up at the entrance. Waiting inside the sliding doors are the Psychiatric Nurse and intake staff as the security team assist in transporting Rob from the ambulance into the emergency room. The nurse, observing the behavior instructs the officers to bring him who into the evaluation room where he will be transferred onto a hospital stretcher and put in six point restraints. After reviewing the incident report then allowing time for Rob to get settled into the room the nurse goes in to begin her triage.

"Hello Mr. Remington, my name is Nurse Cynthia. I am the nurse here today. Can you tell me what is going on today?" she asks. As the nurse waits patiently for Rob Jr's response he looks up at her appearing calmer than in the previous hour.

"I have a drinking problem and I need some help. I promised my mom that I would go get help for my drinking problem. I went to the Care Unit Center to get help and they said they couldn't help me. So I had to tell them that I was going to kill myself just to get help. So that's why I am here," he says. The nurse curious of his drinking problem and his suicidal comments inquires.

"So Mr. Remington, do you still feel suicidal right now?" ask the Nurse. Rob Jr. looks at the nurse smiling.

"No I don't feel suicidal, but I feel that I'm going to die if I don't get help for my alcohol problem," says Rob. Probing more before writing her triage notes and consulting with the Psychiatrist who is on call, the nurse stares at Rob curiously.

"Mr. Remington, how long have you been drinking?" she asks. Rob Jr., struggling to adjust to the physical restraints he was placed in tries to explain his history with alcohol.

"I've been drinking wine heavily since my dad lied to me five years ago after promising me that would take over his company when he retires," says Rob. Curious to what he's alluding to the nurse probes with more questions.

"What does your dad have to do with your drinking problem?" asks the Nurse. Rob responds angrily

"Well, when he lied to me and hired this black guy I became very depressed. Then I started drinking heavily to deal with my pain," says Rob. Typing in her triage notes, the nurse ponders her thoughts and looks up at Rob Jr.

"So going back to your thoughts of suicide, do you have a plan?" asks the Nurse. Rob, starting to get more upset with the series of questions the nurse was asking gets very quiet in an act of defiance.

"So I'm hearing that you're willing to get help for your alcohol abuse problem, right?" says the Nurse. Rob Jr. responds immediately.

"Yes, that's what I was trying to do before they brought me to this dungeon," says Rob. The nurse gets up from her chair, close her tablet and began to walk away.

"Mr. Remington I will be back. I need to talk to the social worker and the doctor, okay?" she says assuring Rob that someone will be here to talk to you. Rob nods affirmatively still struggling with the physical restraints he was placed in when he arrived. Going into the consultation room the nurse sits down with the social worker and the resident psychiatrist on duty to explain her conversation with the patient during her triage.

"Robert Remington Jr. is a thirty year old Caucasian male whose chief complaint is alcohol dependency. He arrived to PES via the police as a violent mental demanding to be admitted at the Care Unit and then threatening suicide. Patient denies feeling suicidal at this time. He states that he mentioned suicide in order to get admitted to the Care Unit. When he was denied admission, he became very volatile and started pacing in the lobby at the care Unit. It was reported that the patient was kicking furniture causing a disturbance which led to the police being called. After being transported to Psychiatric Emergency Services patient states that he has been drinking wine every day for the last five years. Patient blames his dad for his alcohol problems, stating that his dad lied to him about taking over the company that he owns. He made reference to dad hiring a black guy in his position. According to the patient his bad relationship with his dad is what led him to continue his substance abuse. Patient is very much disheveled and smells of alcohol which leads me to believe that he had been drinking before arriving to the Care Unit. His vital were stable but blood pressure was a little elevated. The doctor after reviewing Rob's medical chart gets up out of his chair to speak with Rob as part of his psychiatric evaluation. Entering the observation room the doctor introduces himself to Rob Jr.

"Hello Mr. Remington, my name is Dr. Norris. I want to take a few minutes to talk with you," says the doctor. Rob raises his head up to get a clearer view of the doctor.

"No offense doc, but can you just call me Rob? I hate my last name," says Rob.

"No problem Rob. The nurse informed me why you're here and some of the issues you are having so I won't burden you with that. However, I need to ask you some more questions. How many meals do you eat a day?" asks Dr. Norris. Rob stares at the doctor.

"I eat once a day," says Rob. Curious why Rob isn't eating more the doctor inquires.

"I am curious to why aren't you eating more on a daily basis?" says Dr. Norris. Rob responds sarcastically.

"Because the halfway house where I stay only serves meals two times a day and I don't eat that slop they serve for breakfast. They put us out at nine o'clock in the morning and we are on our own until dinner time," says Rob. Dr. Norris shakes his head while taking notes from Rob's conversation with him.

"Are you having any stomach pains throughout the day?" ask the doctor.

"Not so much hunger pains but sharp pains when I can't get a drink. Sometimes they have me so bent over at times that I feel like I'm going to die!" says Rob. The doctor feels the area and notices an unusual lump below his bellybutton that is a cause of concern for the doctor.
"Now, I want you to take several deep breaths while I feel where you are experiencing the pain," says the doctor. As Rob takes several deep breaths the doctor continues to examine.

"Rob, just relax I'll be back, I need to talk to the nurse," he says. Dr. Norris summons the nurse to call the floor and have Robert Remington Jr. admitted to 8 WEST with a diagnosis of depression with manic episodes of suicidal ideation caused by alcoholism. As the nurse calls the floor she shares of a new admission to the nurse.

"We are admitting Robert Remington Jr. to 8 WEST with a diagnosis of depression with manic episodes of suicidal ideation caused by alcoholism. I also want the patient to also have a medical consult for severe gastrointestinal infection and a workup to rule out any early stages of cirrhosis of the liver," says the Nurse. Forty minutes later, Rob was informed that he will be admitted to the hospital. He was taken to his room on 8WEST.

Chapter 6

Entering the high rise office building where the Remington Corporation is located Aaron is surprised to see a crowd of local media reporters outside the corporate office. Not realizing they were there to interview him for achieving the Remington Corporation's first Fortune 500 Award. Attempting to avoid the media blitz Aaron tries to walk through the stream of reporters and cameras but is stopped by reporters seeking to interview him. After continuous request to be interviewed Aaron honor their request.

"Mr. Williams, I am Matt Lynch from Channel 4 News. I heard you were responsible for getting the Remington Corporation the Fortune 500 Foundation award. Can you speak on it?" asks the Reporter.

"Yes, I was able to secure a major bids from several national companies that got us placed on the Fortune 500 Foundation list. But it wouldn't have been possible without the leadership of the President and CEO Robert Remington Sr." says Aaron.

"Michael Young of Channel 7 News, Mr. Williams I heard you were the only African American working for the Remington Corporation. How does that feel for a corporation that has a long history of not hiring minorities to have you take them to Fortune 500 status?" he asks.

"Well, I can't speak of its history. I have been here at the Remington Corporation for six years and I haven't had or seen any problems as it relates to race. I think it is was just a matter of time before those numbers would change as it relates to hiring more minorities if they are qualified," says Aaron Watching the gathering of reporters from her office window lining up to interview Aaron, Kimberly immediately gets very upset and storms out of her office and goes into Mr. Remington's office unannounced slamming the door behind her. Mr. Remington looks up surprised at Kimberly's antics and stares at her.

"What in the hell is going on Kimberly?" asks Remington. Kimberly leans over Remington's office desk literally screaming at him in anger. "What the hell are you doing about Aaron?" she asks. Confused to what she is talking about Remington stares at Kimberly giving her a disturbing look.

"What are you talking about?' says Remington.

"Robert, what in the hell am I supposed to do with all the local media in the hallway blocking the entrance to your business interviewing Aaron about what he did to get your corporation to Fortune 500 status? Why you allowing Aaron to have all these interviews? Why you just sitting back in your office letting Aaron get all of the attention for something you should be getting the credit for? You built this business from the ground up to where it is today. Shouldn't they be interviewing you as the owner of the Remington Corporation? What you have to say about this entire media blitz that's going on? I'm not able to do my work because of all the noise outside of my office. In fact you promised your son that when you retired that he would take over the corporation. It's unfortunate that you don't even have a relationship with your own flesh and blood. You ever thought about the reason why your son is having problems? Did you ever think that your son turned to alcohol because he had a void in his life? Robert did you ever consider your son's feelings or point of view? How do you think he felt when he found out that you hired a black man to the position that was promised to him? Now look at what is happening now! A black man who is now trying to take over your company. Aaron is getting all of the attention for the Fortune 500 award your corporation received. It's a damn shame! Oh by the way, I fail to mention that Aaron is receiving a lot of phone calls and messages since his recognition. I suggest that you check his phone calls and voice mails. I believe he is masterminding a takeover of your corporation. Don't lose every damn thing you worked for Robert!" says Kimberly' As Kimberly slams the door as she leaves out of her boss' office angry. Sitting at his desk in shock at Kimberly's comments against Aaron. Remington stares out of his bay window looking over the downtown skyscraper. Moments later Remington calls Kimberly back into his office to share a few words with her. As Kimberly walks back into the office still angry takes a seat and stares at her boss waiting to hear what he has to say.

"Kimberly, I need to tell you this and I will not say it to you again. Aaron is an employee of high character and there is no reason for me to believe that he will attempt to take over my corporation. In fact I see him as a person who has brought value to my business operation as a professional. And yes, he is the reason why we reached Fortune 500 status. That's all I have to say to you about that. As far as I am concerned this will be our last conversation about what you feel about Aaron," says Remington. As Mr. Remington ask Kimberly to excuse herself from his office, he turns his chair Going to her office very disappointed and realizing that Mr. Remington will be out of town on business, Kimberly plots a plan. A plan to bring in a rogue technician to cross the corporation phone wires into Aaron's office where she can receive his phone calls and voice mails. As Mr. Remington leaves his office and goes to the elevator Kimberly immediately goes into her phone directory to find the number of Ralph Lowell, a close friend who knows of a rogue technician who previously worked in telecommunications as an installer. Getting up from her desk and locking her door Kimberly calls Ralph.

"Good morning Ralph, this is Kimberly. I need a big favor from you. You know that young man who formerly worked in telecommunications that you introduced me to several months ago? I may need his services here at the Remington Corporation," says Kimberly. Hearing Kimberly's request Ralph responds.

"What's going on at the Remington Corporation?" asks Ralph. Kimberly responds immediately expressing her anger.

"We have this black man Aaron Williams who is trying to take over the Remington Corporation and I am not going to let this shit happen. Robert Remington is saying how good of a guy he is. He's been getting all the attention and lately from the media because of this Fortune 500 Award that the Remington Corporation received this weekend. The media has been here and he thinks he is running this damn place. He is also getting a lot of phone calls here from some prominent people in this city. I believe he is trying to take over the corporation. I need to know who he is talking to so I can bring him down," she says. After hearing Kimberly being very upset Ralph responds.

"His name is David. How soon do you need him Kimberly? He's only a phone call away," says Ralph. Kimberly anxiously replies"

"Well I need him this weekend to do a job," says Kimberly.

"Let me give David a call Kimberly. I will call you as soon as I hear from him," says Ralph. Thirty minutes later Ralph calls Kimberly to inform her that he has arranged a meeting with David at six o'clock at Mario's Italian Restaurant on Main Street this evening.

"That's great! I will be there! Thank you Ralph for hooking me up," says Kimberly before hanging up the phone. Later that evening Kimberly is seen at Mario's Italian Restaurant, a small speak easy restaurant establishment known for providing businessmen to dine and make deals. Sitting in the dimly lit corner table of the restaurant, Kim looks out the window anxiously waiting for David to arrive. Moments later a Caucasian man around forty years old walks into the restaurant looking around suspiciously. Feeling that he is the one she is supposed to be meeting Kimberly raises her hand like a prostitute on the street and flags down David directing him to her table. Recognizing the hand signal David comes back to the corner table where Kimberly greets him.

"Hello David I'm Kimberly whom Ralph referred you to. Have a seat," she says. As David sits down Kimberly pulls her chair closer to the table to have more privacy.

"What would you like to drink? Everything is on me," says Kimberly. David somewhat modest but needing a drink takes Kimberly up on her offer.

"I'll take a Long Island Ice Tea please with little ice," says David. Immediately Kim calls the waiter over to take their drink orders.

"We would like two Long Island Ice Tea double shots of everything with little ice," says Kimberly. As the waiter takes their orders and goes back to the bar to request their drinks Kim speaks softly so no one can hear their conversation.

"David, I remember meeting you several months ago at the party for Ralph. When we met you said you were in telecommunications and if I needed your services to call. Well, I need your services now! And I'll take care of you financially," says Kimberly. David stares at Kimberly and responds.

"What job do you want me to do?" asks David.

"We have a problem with an employee at the office that we need to resolve. We think he is undermining the company and we need to get to the bottom of it. I need for you to cross some of the telephone wires between offices so we can find out who he is calling and who is calling into the office speaking to him and leaving voicemails. Can you do it?" asks Kimberly. Looking at Kimberly smiling David responds.

"I can make it happen, however it may take me a couple of hours because there is a lot involved," says David. Kimberly looks around the restaurant making sure no one is listening in on their conversation.

"Can you make it happen this weekend?" ask Kimberly.

"I can make anything happen if the price is right," says David laughing. Stopping the conversation observing the waiter coming back to the table with the drinks Kimberly pauses. As the waiter places the drinks on the table, Kimberly gives the waiter her credit card.

"You can go ahead bring us the bill," says Kimberly. As the waiter leaves Kimberly reaches inside her purse and pulls out an envelope with money in it.

"I'll pay you twenty-five hundred now. And twenty-five hundred after you complete the job," says Kimberly smiling. David opens the envelope and looks at the cash money smiles and responds.

"Deal, I can be there Saturday morning at ten o'clock sharp," says David. Kim hands David a business card with the address of the Remington Corporation.

"I will meet you at my office around ten o'clock Saturday morning," says Kimberly. After shaking hands David and Kimberly get out of their chairs and walks toward the restaurant exit. The following Saturday morning Kimberly is in her office looking out the window wait for the technician David to show up to cross the wires in Aaron's office to her office. As it becomes close to ten o'clock Kim hear the opening of the elevators in the hallway. She anxiously goes to the door and notices David getting off the elevator and greets him. David adjusts his tool belt he is shown the communication room at the end of the hallway. Needing to know which offices will be affected by the wiring of the phones David is taken to Aaron and Kimberly's offices. After getting the serial numbers off the phones David goes back to the communication room where there is a mass of wiring and starts using his pen light needle scanner to make sure the lines are active. Once he realizes they are active he begins to splice and add additional wiring to Aaron and Kimberly's phone lines to have Aaron's calls and voicemails to be also transmitted Kimberly's phone. Sealing the telephone wires with a plastic coating, David goes to Kimberly's office to add a device to her phone to activate the calls. After completing the job David smiles and looks at Kimberly.

"The job is done. You should be able to receive all of his calls and voicemails," says David.
After receiving the good news Kimberly reaches in her pocket and hands David a folded envelope containing the twenty-five hundred owed after completion thanking him for his service.

"David, you're a life saver or should I say a corporation saver. What you did today should avoid any illegal activities going on in this corporation by this employee who is attempting to take over the corporation," says Kimberly. Kim walks David to the elevator and thanks him.

Chapter 7

Bright and early Monday morning Aaron arrives to work happy to see the absence of the media who crowded the lobby last week. Walking past the reception desk he greets Camille in his usual manner.

"Good Morning Camille, have I received any calls this morning?" asks Aaron. Camille looks at Aaron with a tired expression on her face.

"Are you kidding me? Since I been here I have sent seven messages to your phone, says Camille. Walking to his office and unlocking the door, Aaron sits his briefcase down and reaches over to his phone to check his voice mail. Also surprised at the volume of calls he has received, Aaron is anxious to listen to his voice messages. Pressing his telephone keypad, Aaron starts listening to the messages.

"You have five new messages. To hear your messages, press one. Aaron presses one.

"First message received Monday 5:10 a.m. from an undisclosed number. I got word that the shipment is set to arrive around two o'clock. Where do you want the shipment to be dropped off? Give me a call. This is the shipment of Cocaine and Meth to be there at ten o'clock so the drop off have to be secure. Aaron, shocked yet confused of the message and why is it coming to his voice mail becomes very nervous and concerned. Aaron presses the keypad again to hear the next voice message.

"Next message received Monday at 6:37 a.m. from an undisclosed number. I got your message about where you're going to meet me to our agreed location to drop off my money. I will be here at noon to pick up my fifty thousand dollars. Talk to you later. Aaron, hearing of the alleged illegal drug trafficking going on at the Remington Corporation becomes very afraid and nervous. Especially since it was sent to his office phone voice message starts to panic and calls his wife. As Aaron waits for his wife to answer the phone he has second thoughts about calling her about this criminal activity thinking that the F.B.I. may have his phones lines tapped. Starting to feel ill, scared and paranoid about all that is going on Aaron decides to go home early. After speaking briefly to his wife without giving her much information, Aaron grabs his briefcase, turns his office lights out as he leaves. As Aaron walks pass Camille's desk he speaks.

"Camille, I'm going home for the day. I'm not feeling well," says Aaron. Camille realizing that Aaron has only been in his office for an hour is curious to what is wrong.

"Aaron what's wrong? You seemed okay when you came in this morning?" said Camille. Avoiding eye contact with Camille responds.

"I just think it's a virus. I'll probably be okay tomorrow. Please let Mr. Remington know that I left early because I wasn't feeling well. I'll talk to you later," says Aaron. As Aaron arrives home surprising his wife as he walks in the family room where she is reading a novel.

"Aaron, why are you home so early? Is everything okay?" asks Asia. Aaron pauses and takes a deep breath.

"Well, not really," said Aaron. As Asia notices that her husband appears to be in a panic state stares at him. She goes over and holds his hand and inquires.

"What's the problem baby?" asks Asia. Sitting next to her husband seeing a look of fear in his eyes Asia gets concerned. Aaron looks up at his wife in disappointment and cries.

"Baby, the man we thought was a very good and honest man is a criminal," says Aaron. Asia shocked at Aaron's comments but still unsure who he is talking about replies nervously.

"Who are you talking about Aaron?" says Asia. Aaron stares at his wife forcing himself to divulge information.

"I think it is Mr. Remington," said Aaron. Asia hearing about Mr. Remington's possible association to criminal activity cringes.

"Aaron, where did you get this information?" said Asia.

"When I arrived at the office Camille informed me that I had a few voice mails before she got to work. I went into my office and checked my voice mails as I normally do before starting my day. When I retrieved my messages I was getting it shocked me. The first one was a man leaving a message about a shipment of cocaine that was set to arrive at 10:00 a.m. Then there was a second message about where the money supposed to be picked up in the amount of fifty thousand dollars. When I heard those messages I got scared baby. I felt sick to my stomach and unsafe. I didn't know what to do at that moment so I decided to come home. I don't know why I was receiving those voicemails," said Aaron. Shocked over Aaron's revelation of his recent disclosure Asia stares at him.

"So, what are you going to do that you know of this information?" asks Asia.

"I don't know Asia. How do I report this to the police? I don't know how much influence Mr. Remington has over the local police," says Aaron. Asia pauses and puts her hand on her husband's shoulder for comfort.

"Aaron, how do you not report suspicious criminal activity once you know about it? What if the police find out that you have been withholding criminal activity and information? They can either charge you with obstruction of justice or tampering with evidence if you tried to hide or erase it," says Asia. Aaron immediately gets up and nervously paces the family room floor confused of what to do with his dilemma.

"Asia I don't know what to do! What should I do?" he asks Asia. Asia gets up and takes her husband's hands and stands in front of him being sympathetic to his concern.

"I think we should go talk to Pastor Wright for prayer and understanding. He always been the person we have went to here on this earth that has shown us the way" says Asia. Aaron gives his wife a hug and a kiss for understanding his plight and responds.

"You're right. Let me call Pastor and see if he is available today," says Aaron. As Aaron pulls out his cell phone, he calls Pastor Wright. After several rings Pastor Wright answers in a pleasant greeting.

"Hello, this is Pastor Vincent Wright, may I help you?" he says.

"Hello Pastor Wright this is Aaron Williams how are you?" asks Aaron. Pastor Wright replies.

"How are you Aaron and how is your wife?" ask the Pastor. Aaron responds to Pastor Wright's question and the reason he is calling.

"The wife and I are doing well, but I called to seek your consultation on another matter that I'm dealing with at work. Is it possible that Asia and I could come over and speak with you today?" asks Aaron. The Pastor sensing that there are problems going on in the family responds quickly.

"Sure Aaron, I am available in the next hour. Just call me when you arrive," says the Pastor. After confirming the time with his wife, Aaron responds to Pastor.

"We will see you in an hour Pastor," says Aaron.

"I'll talk to both of you soon," says Pastor Wright. Happy that Pastor can meet with them, Aaron looks at Asia and smiles. He gives Asia a hug and thanks her for understanding his plight they prepare themselves for visiting Pastor Wright. Asia smiles and speaks softly to Aaron.

"You know God has got us through many storms during our marriage. He will surely get us through this one. We just have to believe that God will get us through this one," said Asia.

Arriving at the office of Pastor Wright, Aaron and Asia is greeted by Pastor Wright who cordially invites them inside and offers them a seat. After embracing both Asia and Aaron and they are settled, Pastor Wright starts off with a prayer.

"Our Father, which art in heaven, hallowed be thy name, thy kingdom come, thy will be done, on earth as it is in heaven, give us this day, our daily bread and forgive us our trespasses, as we forgive those who trespass against us, and lead us not into temptation, but deliver us from evil, for thine is the kingdom, and the power, and the glory, forever, and Amen!" says Pastor Wright.

As Aaron and Asia responds saying Amen after the prayer, Pastor Wright looks up at them as he prepare to hear what both Aaron and Asia want to discuss with him today. Aaron looks nervously at Pastor Wright and clears his throat before sharing his experience.

"Well Pastor, I went to work this morning as I normally do and after greeting our Receptionist Camille and asking if I had received any phone messages she informed me that I had. In fact, she informed me that I received quite a few voice messages. Realizing that I don't normally receive many voicemails, I immediately went to my office to retrieve them. As I activated my voice messages on my office phone I heard two messages that implicated that someone at the Remington Corporation being involved in the illegal drug distribution trafficking ring. It mentioned about a shipment of drugs, more specifically cocaine and meth coming into our city today. I went to the following voice message and there was a man on the voice message who said that he would be at a location to pick up the fifty thousand dollars. From whom I don't know but he was confirming the delivery. He said that he would be there at noon to pick up the fifty thousand dollars. I was thinking that the message was meant for Mr. Remington. I became very nervous and immediately called my wife and left work that morning. I informed Camille, our Receptionist that I was sick and going home. As I drove home I struggled with my decision as to what I should do about those voice mails regarding illegal drug trafficking and calls coming to the Remington Corporation. Should I not say anything and keep my lucrative job and the honor of getting the Remington Corporation to Fortune 500 status? Or should I be a whistle blower and risk losing my job or possibly risking my life? Pastor, the reason why I'm struggling with my decision is just last weekend Asia and I went to New York City with the Mr. Remington who is the President and CEO to receive the prestigious Fortune 500 Award. Plus prior to that Mr. Remington gave me a bonus performance check in the amount of fifty thousand dollars. And if he is involved in illegal drug trafficking I would be very upset," says Aaron. As Pastor Wright, hearing Aaron explaining his dilemma pauses to reflect on some of the things that Aaron has shared. He looks at both Aaron and Asia. As he moves his chair closer to them Pastor Wright ask if they can all hold hands with each other before praying.

"Aaron and Asia, I don't know how much I can assist you emotionally with your current situation but I can sure give you my professional and spiritual opinion. But right now before we pray I want to speak to you as your Pastor by advising you to tell the truth. You must speak truth over power. You cannot partake in a series of corruption with the enemy even though they're giving you opportunities you never had before. You must do what's right in the eyes of God. You must eradicate out sin even in your workplace. I suggest that you notify the authorities immediately. Imagine, anytime that justice is not served, innocent people are victimized. I can guarantee you that if you don't report this illegal activity within 48 hours somebody possibly will be murdered on our streets. They can be killed because of a drug deal gone bad, drug overdose or territorial control. You are going through a worldly storm right now. First, you trust in God. I have a friend that works for the DEA. I can call and let her know what's going on. I also recommend that you not go to work right now because of the implications that the investigation may cause you in the workplace. I strongly suggest that you take a personal leave. Are you willing to speak truth to power Aaron?" says Pastor Wright. Aaron stares at Pastor Wright and nods in agreement. Pastor motions with his hands for Aaron and Asia to stand up and form a circle, hold hands and bow their heads in prayer.

"Heavenly Father, as we leave out on our journey of truth, I ask that you protect us from the enemy. Allow us to speak with righteousness and love in the deliverance of your word. As the bible says in Jeremiah 29:11-13 which says. For I know the plans I have for you, declares the Lord, plans to prosper you and not harm you, plans to give you hope and a future. Then you will call upon me and come and pray to me, and

I will listen to you. You will seek me and find me with all your heart. Amen," says Pastor Wright.

"God has a plan for you if you just keep believing. You are facing obstacles in your life. I want you to trust and lean on God. He will never fail you. I've been pastoring for twenty-three years, and I know what God will do. Aaron, are you willing to speak to my friend down at the Drug Enforcement Agency about your situation?" ask Pastor Wright.

"Yes I am," said Aaron. Moments later Pastor Wright takes out his cell phone and calls Agent Blake at the DEA office.

"Hello, this is Pastor Vincent Wright. I would like to speak with Agent Monica Blake.

"Just a moment please. May I ask who is calling?" says the Receptionist.

"Yes, this is Pastor Vincent Wright," he says. Moments later Agent Blake answers the phone.

"Agent Blake may I help you?" she asks.

"Agent Blake, Pastor Wright. How are you?" he asks.

"I am doing well Pastor, how are you?" asks the Agent.

"I am doing well. However, I have a couple of my church members who have a situation and may need to talk with you. You have any-time this afternoon where we could come down to your office?" asks Pastor Wright.

"I have time available right now if you can come to my office," says Agent Blake.

"That's great, their names are Aaron and Asia Williams and we will be there in approximately fifteen minutes," says the Pastor. Arriving at the Drug Enforcement Agency with Pastor Wright, Aaron and Asia walks into the office reception area where they are greeted by DEA Receptionist.

"Hello, my name is Pastor Wright and I'm here with Aaron and Asia Williams. I spoke earlier with Agent Blake and she is expecting us," says the Pastor.

"Yes, Agent Blake informed me you would be coming to see her. Have a seat and I will let her know that you are here," says the

Receptionist. As Pastor, Aaron and Asia takes a seat, moments later Agent Blake comes out to the reception area and greets her guest and encourage them to come to her office.

"Hello, Pastor Wright and guest, come on to my office" says the Agent. As Pastor Wright, Aaron and Asia follows Agent Blake to her office and takes a seat, Pastor Wright does an introduction.

"Agent Blake this is Aaron and Asia Williams. They came to me seeking advice on a serious issue that Aaron is dealing with at his job. I would like for Aaron to share with you, what's going on as it relates to the corporation he works for," says Pastor Wright. Gathering his thoughts before speaking, Aaron looks at the Agent and speaks.

"Agent Blake, as Pastor Wright said my name is Aaron Williams, Senior Executive of Operations at the Remington Corporation that's located in the Pyramid Office Towers in downtown Chapel. This morning I arrived at the corporation and after greeting the Receptionist, I asked her if I had received any messages. She informed me that I had numerous messages on my voice mail before I arrived. I went into my office to retrieve my voice messages and what I heard was very alarming the messages that I received mentioned of a drug shipment that was going to be dropped off somewhere in Chapel. I believe the message was for someone who works at the Remington Corporation. The first message mentioned of a shipment of drugs that was arriving this morning. The second message mentioned about a location where the money was going to be picked up. It mentioned a pickup of fifty thousand dollars. I got afraid and very nervous and told the Receptionist that I was going home early because I was sick," says Aaron nervously. As Agent Blake starts typing on her laptop the information that Aaron shared, then she looks up at him and speaks.

"Did you save the voice messages Mr. Williams?" asks Agent Blake.

"Yes I did. Would you like to hear them?" asks Aaron. Inquisitive about the messages Agent Blake acknowledged the request. After hearing the messages from Aaron's phone Agent Blake felt that there was enough information to initiate a drug investigation. Curious to the direction of the voice messages, Agent Blake questions Aaron.

"Aaron, you have any idea why these voice mails were coming to your office phone?" inquires Agent Blake. Aaron shakes his head and responds.

"I have no idea why they came to my phone. I think that they got the phone lines crossed and it came to my phone by mistake," says Aaron. As Agent Blake continues to type information on her computer, she looks at Pastor Wright and Aaron and responds.

"This situation appears to be very serious. I will turn this matter over to one of our Investigation Team and they will do their internal investigation. Mr. Williams, what I will need from you is your mobile number in case we need more information as I am sure we will. I will ask that while we are doing our investigating that you do not share any information with any of your co-workers or friends. It could seriously interfere with our investigation," says Agent Blake.

Collectively Aaron, Pastor Wright and Asia nod in agreement with the Agent's request. As the Agent prepares to walk them back to the reception area she shakes their hand and reassures them that they will follow up with their investigation. After going to their vehicles, Aaron and Asia thank Pastor Wright for his support and prayers along with accompanying them to the authorities.

Chapter 8

Getting off the elevator appearing exhausted from a busy weekend Kimberly slowly opens the door and walks into her office. As she gets settled in her chair looks at her phone and realizes that she hasn't received any voicemail messages directed to Aaron's office. However looking at the control center she notices that Aaron has received quite a few voicemail messages this morning.

"Wow! It appears that our new black celebrity is getting a lot of attention this morning. Let me check on who is calling him," says Kimberly. Pressing the device that David connected to her phone to listen to Aaron's phone messages she listens to some disturbing messages that wasn't meant for him.

"First message received Monday 5:10 a.m. from an undisclosed number. I got word that the shipment is set to arrive around ten o'clock. Where do you want the shipment to be dropped off? Give me a call. This is the shipment of Cocaine and Meth to be there at ten o'clock so the drop off has to be secure. Where you want me to distribute it? Give me a call?" Kimberly, shocked and feeling nervous that the voicemail that was intended for her were sent to Aaron's phone. Curious to what other messages Aaron has received Kim presses the device that was placed to listen to other messages that were sent to Aaron's phone.

"Next message received Monday at 6:37 a.m. from an undisclosed number. I got your message about where you're going to meet me to our agreed location to drop off my money. I will be there at noon to pick up my fifty thousand dollars. Talk to you later." Moments later Kim goes into the reception area to speak to Camille.

"Good morning Camille has Aaron been here?" asks Kimberly looking nervous.

"Yes, Aaron was here but he went home ill about an hour ago," said Camille. Curious to Aaron's so called illness, Kimberly probes Camille for more information.

"Did he say what was wrong?" asks Kimberly.

"Yes, he said he thinks he has some type of virus," said Camille. Kimberly suspecting that Aaron may have heard the voicemails and decided to go home pauses then smiles at Camille.

"Camille, what time are you taking your lunch break?" asks Kimberly.

"I'll be going to lunch in about five minutes. You need me to stay around?" she ask. Kimberly responds immediately.

"Oh no Camille, you go and enjoy your lunch. I was only asking to see if you wanted to go to lunch with me," says Kimberly.

"No thanks, I'm meeting a friend who is buying lunch," says Camille. Kimberly smiles politely at Camille as she leaves out of the Reception area. As Camille gets on the elevator on her way to lunch Kimberly looks around to make sure no one was in the offices. She goes in her office and locks the door and places a call on her cell phone. After several rings Ralph answers the phone.

"Hello Ralph!" he answers.

"Ralph, where is that son of a bitch you sent me? He screwed up our phone lines and got my calls going to someone else" says Kimberly extremely upset. Hearing Kimberly literally screaming through her phone demanding answers from him, Ralph tries to calm down Kimberly down.

"He told me about the money you paid him for completing the job," says Ralph.

"Call him now and tell him to get his ass down here to put these telephone wires back the way they were now!" says Kimberly screaming and upset. Ralph realizing the seriousness of what has happened reassures Kimberly that he will get in touch with David. Kimberly realizing that the damage is already done, figures that Aaron is now aware of the drug trafficking operation at the Remington Corporation. Slamming her phone down, Kimberly ponders angrily the worst case scenario and her next move. She picks up her cell phone and calls a person who is a hit man known in the community to have Aaron murdered. As Kimberly dials a number she has stored in her personal cell phone.

"Joe, may I help you?" he says.

"Hey Joe this is Kimberly. What's up?" she says. Joe takes a pause to realize who was calling him and responds.

"Hey Kimberly, what's up?" says Joe.

"I need your help!" says Kimberly.

"Let me take one guess, somebody rolled you for your money now you want them dead, right?" says Joe laughing.

"No Joe, I got a co-worker that knows too much and I need him taken out. What you charging these days to do a job?" asks Kimberly. Joe, feeling to need more information, probes Kimberly further regarding the person she wants dead.

"What happened?" asks Joe.

"We got this black guy who works at the Remington Corporation who is trying to take over the company. Since he helped the Remington Corporation get to Fortune 500 status he is beyond himself. He is acting as if he is the President and CEO. Then he started getting all kinds of calls and meeting with people as if he is getting to take over the corporation. So when Mr. Remington wouldn't do anything about it I'm taking it upon myself to find out why he was getting all these calls. That's when I called a friend of mine who introduced me to rogue phone technician. I paid him to cross the phone wires at the Remington Corporation. That way his calls would also come to my office phone. Over the weekend this rogue technician came to the offices and crossed the phone wires so that his calls would come to my office. Well, this son of a bitch somehow crossed the wires where my calls end up going to his phone. He now has information that about some things that I'm doing that is illegal and will get me in serious trouble with the corporation and the law if they found out what I was doing. It's serious enough Joe that I need for him to be taken out immediately.

"When you talk about immediately when are you talking about? Where you talking about me taking him out at? And most importantly, what are you willing to pay for me to do the job?" asks Joe.

"The answer to your first question is soon as possible. The answer to your second question is a place we can arrange this hit. And your last question is negotiable. But money won't be a problem. I can get that from the Remington bank account. And I want to cover this up so I won't be a suspect. Let's do the job in the parking garage here at the Remington Corporation," says Kimberly. Hearing Kimberly's answers to his questions Joe responds.

"That's fine with me Kimberly. I just need to know when and what time. By it being in a public parking garage I will have to use my silencer and know where he parks his car. Also, we need to know where we can meet so you can drop off my money to do the job," says Joe. Kimberly immediately responds.

"Let's meet this evening at six o'clock at Mario's Italian Restaurant. How much are you charging me to do the job?" she asks.

"Kimberly, you know we're the only profession in the world that doesn't get into that inflation bullshit like gas prices, food and prostitutes. My price stays the same. Five thousand down then five thousand after the job is done," says Joe. Kimberly responds.

"You know I got shanked by a rogue technician who crossed the wires wrong. That is the reason I'm asking you" says Kimberly. Joe responds humorously to Kimberly's comments.

"Well Kimberly, that's what happens when you hire an amateur to do a professional job. I will meet you at Mario's Italian Restaurant at six o'clock this evening," says Joe.

"That a deal, see you then," says Kimberly. Kimberly hangs up the phone feeling very relieved about her plan.

Chapter 9

As Robert Jr. prepares to be discharged from his twenty-one-day stay at the Care Unit after spending three days at University Hospital Psychiatric, Robert Jr. is overly surprised to see Deena and Sarah in the lobby. Deena, carrying a bouquet of flowers, balloons and a card approaches Rob and gives him a hug as well as his mom. Rob, looking well after three weeks of treatment smiles.

"How did you know I was getting out?" says Rob Jr. Deena looks at him sarcastically and smiles.

"Like there is no way to check on you crazy. All we had to do was call the information desk and tell them who we are and they would have updated us on your status. I was checking up on you every week even though I wasn't making visits. Remember, I'm your sister and she is your mother right?" says Deena smiling. As Deena and Sarah starts laughing Rob gives them a hug and gets very emotional.

"Deena, I never thought you cared for me, especially since I became an alcoholic," says Rob Jr. Deena takes Rob Jr. hands and places them in hers and smiles.

"Rob, regardless of what you have been through I am always going to be your sister and I love you. You have disappointed me at times but I never lost my faith and love for you. Mom and I got some good news for you," she says smiling looking at their mom.

"That's great, I haven't heard any good news in so long that I started to believe that my life was nothing but bad news," said Rob. Deena looks at her mom again smiling before responding.

"Mom, why don't you tell Rob the good news?" says Deena. Sarah looks at her son with a glowing smile and speaks.

"Rob, I want to share with you that I am now cancer free! I had a checkup this week with my Oncologist and he said I am now free of breast cancer," says Sarah. As Rob smiles while tearing up and gives his mom a hug, she shares some more good news to her son.

"The other good news is that you will no longer have to stay at that halfway house. Deena and I have leased you a furnished apartment with your rent paid for the next six months until you can find a job. We also started you a bank account in your name," said Sarah. Rob, extremely elated about his mom being cancer free and that she and Deena had found him a new apartment breaks down in tears. He looks at both of them in sincere appreciation and smiles.

"You didn't have to do this for me. I am ready to get my life together and do what's right. But I realize that I am going to need your help," says Rob.

"Well Rob, that help starts now because we are going to take you over to your new furnished apartment not too far from where we live. We have stocked your refrigerator and cabinets with plenty of food. And we also got you a bus card for the month. In addition, we spoke to Alcohol Anonymous and they are getting you a sponsor so they can help you in your recovery," said Deena. As Rob prepares to walk out of the hospital holding on to his mom, to the parking lot the hospital staff smiles and waves at them. As Sarah, Deena and Rob Jr. leave the hospital and go to Rob's new furnished apartment, Rob shares a part of him to his mother and sister that they haven't heard from him.

"Mom and Deena, what do you think if I went to dad and ask him to forgive me?" said Rob Jr. Very shocked to hear what Rob said, Deena almost caused a wreck on the freeway causing her to pull over on the side of the road.

"Rob, are you serious?" asks Deena raising her voice at a high volume as she looks back at Rob who is sitting in the back seat. Hearing Deena, Rob responds immediately.

"Yes, I'm dead serious but I would need you and mom with me when I go ask for forgiveness," says Rob. Since I been in rehab and off using alcohol my mind started to be clearer and my thoughts have been more coherent. What I was saying about dad was a way to have not focus on my illness. And then when you told me about mom's illness that really sent me spiraling. That is one of the main reasons for going to check myself into rehab and ending up in the psych ward," says Rob. After hearing what she believes is a seriousness in Rob, Sarah speaks out to Rob.

"Rob, if you are serious about speaking with your dad and asking for forgiveness what better time than now. Your dad is at home by himself and because it's the weekend he is not busy. What a great time for you, Deena and I to go over and have a conversation with him," says Sarah. Hearing his mom suggestion, Rob agrees to speak to his dad now instead of later. On that decision, Deena changed directions and heads in the direction of her parents' home to have a conversation with Rob and dad. After a brief drive back to her parent's house Deena before getting out of the car with her mom and Rob ask both if she could pray with them. When she got the okay from both of them she started prayer.

"Dear Heavenly Father, I come to you this afternoon asking that you watch over my brother Rob as well as my dad as they engage in a conversation to mend their problems with each other. As my brother ask for forgiveness Father God, I ask that you watch over all of us as we pray that my dad accept Rob's forgiveness for what he did to him. Amen," says Deena. Getting out of the car, Sarah says that she will speak to her husband prior to their meeting to inform him of what is going on. After going into the house and speaking to her husband Robert Sr. about their son's request to talk to him. After a lengthy conversation with him as to why his son wanted to talk to him and that he wanted to ask him for forgiveness. He at first said no but after a short explanation he decided to hear what Rob Jr. had to say. As Deena and Rob walks into the family room where Robert Sr. is sitting on the sofa, both Deena and Rob greets him to which they got no response. Deena decides to open up the conversation with dad and her brother.

"Dad, as you're aware we are here after Rob decided that he wanted to share some things with you at this time. So I will just have Rob share what he wanted to talk you about," says Deena. Rob, somewhat hesitant and nervous begins to speak.

"Dad, I know it has been difficult for you as a father having to deal with my situation and lifestyle. You invested in me and gave me everything a father could give a son and I failed you. Because of it I became someone you didn't expect. I became a failure as a son as well as an alcoholic. Then to make things worse, I denounce you in front of your family and friends. Things got so bad in my life that I had nowhere to turn. Even my dear sister tried in vain to talk to me and even encourage me to go get help for my alcoholism. She realized that I was a complete drunk. But when things hit rock bottom was when she told me that mom might have breast cancer. With my mom's illness, you losing trust in me and Deena seeing me in my condition, I had no family to turn to who could help me. At that point I has really hit rock bottom. My close friend outside our family verbally read a eulogy involving my death as an alcoholic that really took me under. The next day after leaving your house I went to the Care Unit, a treatment hospital for alcoholics to get treatment or as I told them to dry out. When it seemed that they wasn't going to give me the help I needed I went ballistic in the lobby. They had to call security and I was transported to University Hospital Psychiatric Emergency to get treatment instead of help for my alcohol addiction. Not only did they treat me for my mental health episode but referred me back to the Care Unit where I originally went to get treatment. "Dad, after successfully completing my alcohol treatment program and being discharged, I felt I needed a life change starting with my behaviors after successfully completing my battle with alcohol addiction. And that behavior starts with me. I shared with mom and

Deena as we left the Care Unit that I wanted to see you and ask you for forgiveness. I know forgiveness in my situation is not easy but it is part of my recovery dad. Today I ask you to forgive me for disrespecting you. I have changed my life and promise to never do you no more harm anymore," says Rob Jr. After hearing his son share his comments and ask him for forgiveness, Robert Sr. stares at Rob, gets up from the sofa and goes over and gives him a warm embrace and responds. After hearing his son share his experiences and overcoming his alcohol addiction, Robert Sr. reflects on the past and looks at his son.

"I forgive you son," says Robert as Sarah and Deena comes over and join as a family showing love for each other.

Chapter 10

It's 7:45 a.m. on Tuesday and Joe is sitting quietly in his car in the Pyramid Office Towers Parking Garage adjusting the sights on his semi-automatic high-powered silencer. His burgundy Honda Civic is angled toward the exit accessible to the freeway for a clean getaway. Having a garage access card given to him by Kimberly, Joe mapped out his plan to avoid surveillance cameras covering up his license plates with black plastic making it almost impossible to detect the identity of the vehicle license plate number when he exits the garage. Having everything planned he relaxes while smoking a cigarette waiting for Aaron to arrive in his parking space. As eight o'clock arrives and there is no sign of Aaron or his vehicle Joe gets concerned. Anxiously watching every car that comes on the level of the garage, Joe pulls out another cigarette out of his pocket impatiently awaiting the time to do his job. As a half hour passes and there is no sign of Aaron, Joe gets irritated. Upset he hasn't been able to reach Kim causes increased anxiety. Unbeknownst to Joe and Kimberly Aaron was told to stay home on Monday by DEA Agent Blake while they do their investigation. At nine o'clock and there is no signs of Aaron, Joe decides to leave the garage obviously very upset that he couldn't complete the job.

At 9:30 a.m. six armed federal drug enforcement agents all wearing blue suits ascended walks up to the doors of the Remington Corporation. After several knocks they announce themselves as Drug Enforcement Agents. As four agents walk into the Remington Corporation offices, they speak to Camille who is sitting at her desk in the Reception area. As one of the agent's flashes his badge and shows Camille a court ordered search warrant signed by a Judge. As the agents separate and go through offices Camille gets very nervous, being the only staff present at the time. Moments later, Mr. Remington Sr. arrives at the Remington Corporation and notices the agents in the offices and looks at Camille.

"What in the hell are they doing in my offices?" says Remington. Before Camille could speak to Mr. Remington, the Drug Enforcement Agent in charge responds.

"We are with the Drug Enforcement Agency and we have a court ordered search warrant.to search the property at the Remington Corporation," he says showing Mr. Remington his badge and the court ordered search warrant signed by the Judge.

"What do you mean? I am Robert Remington Sr. President and CEO of the Remington Corporation and I wasn't informed of a search warrant!" he says raising his voice. As Mr. Remington continues to get very emotionally, upset that he is unable to go to his office during the search, he demanded to speak to someone in charge, the agents physically forms a wall not allowing him or no other staff to force their way through the hallway. After about thirty minutes of their search, the DEA agents come back to the reception area with several packages of information that they have seized. Among them were several telephones with their message system attached to them. As the DEA agents are carrying the property out of the Remington Corporation, Mr. Remington looks confused and visibly upset, gets on the phone and calls the Drug Enforcement Agency office. When the Receptionist answers the phone she is greeted rudely by Mr. Remington.

"What in the hell is going on? These damn agents just left my offices at the Remington Corporation and raided my place! We are a Fortune 500 Company! Again, what in the hell is going on? "Mr., Remington shouts out.

"Let me have you speak to the special agent in charge of operations," says the Receptionist.

Moments later Agent Monica Blake answers the call.

"Agent Monica Blake, may I help you?" she says.

"This is Robert Remington Sr. President and CEO of the Remington Corporation and some of your agents just left after raiding my offices. What in the hell is going on?" he asks.

"Mr. Remington, the Drug Enforcement Agency received a court order signed by the Judge to do a legal search on your property today. That was based on a report of a possible drug trafficking operation at the Remington Corporation and the possibility that phone were being used as a form of communication to execute illegal drug transactions," says Agent Blake.

"Where in the hell did you hear this from?" asks Mr. Remington.

"Mr. Remington, we are not at liberty at this time to disclose that information. All I can say is that you will be hearing from us in the near future regarding our findings," says Agent Blake.

After the agents left the premises of the Remington Corporation, local and regional media converge converged in the hallway of the Remington Corporation taking videos and interviewing anyone affiliated with the Remington Corporation. Moments later, Kimberly arrives to the offices surprised to see a large number of media outlets in the hallway. Shocked as what was going on, Kimberly is questioned by reporters asking if she worked at the Remington Corporation. Ignoring their questioning, she walks into the offices and stares at Camille.

"What in the hell is going on Camille?" asks Kimberly. Camille nervously responds.

"The drug enforcement agents just left here with a court ordered search warrant and went through all the offices looking for evidence. They mentioned to Mr. Remington about an illegal drug operation here at the Remington Corporation," says Camille. Kimberly, curious to what they were looking for responds.

"What were they looking for and what did they get Camille?" asks Kimberly nervously.

"All I saw is that they walked out of here with two bags of evidence and two telephones and two voice message systems," said Camille. Immediately after hearing what Camille shared, Kimberly immediately went to her office to see if anything was confiscated. Realizing that some items were taken from her office she began to get very nervous. She leaves her office and goes over to Aaron's office to see if anything was taken from his desk. Realizing that his telephone and messaging system was seized she shakes her head. Moments later without speaking to Camille, Kimberly leaves the offices of the Remington Corporation not telling Camille when she was going to be back. By midday, breaking news of a federal investigation of the Remington Corporation has the city alarmed. Implications of possible federal indictments began to hit the airwaves through television, radio and print media. The city was shocked of the news that the Remington Corporation was being investigated. Sitting at home, Aaron and his wife Asia receives the heart breaking news of the search warrant while watching television. When the news broke regarding the Remington Corporation investigation, they were watching their favorite program. Visibly nervous and very upset, Aaron immediately picks up his cell phone and calls Pastor Wright whom he relies on for advice and support. Aaron, realizing that he will probably be called in as a witness to testify against the Remington Corporation if charges are brought. Unable to reach Pastor Wright, Aaron places his phone on the table and puts his head in his hands then takes a sigh of distress.

"Why is this happening to me? Why?" asks Aaron. Asia looks at her husband sternly speaking in a soft tone.

"Aaron, you know things happen for a reason. I think it's sending us a clear message that regardless of how good things appear to be. If there is any wrong doing it will be revealed in time. Mr. Remington has a good heart as far as being benevolent. Do you think he would do anything like that?" says Asia. Moments later, the doorbell rings that startles both Aaron and Asia. As Aaron gets up from his chair and goes to the door to see whom it may be he raises his voice and inquires.

"Who is it?" he asks.

"We're agents from the Drug Enforcement Administration along with the Chapel Police Department," says the agent. Upon hearing the identification Aaron slowly opens the door.

"Good afternoon, come on in. What is going on?" asks Aaron nervously. Showing their identification as they walk in the agents and the Chapel Police are led to the family room by Aaron where Asia is sitting. Taking a seat and pulling out their notes one of the agents from DEA informs Aaron and his wife Asia of a serious situation involving the Remington Corporation.

"Mr. Williams as you probably have heard, a search warrant was served on the Remington Corporation today. As we continue our investigation we have confirmed information that a murder for hire plot was set up to have you assassinated yesterday. The murder plot was foiled when you didn't show up for work causing the alleged hit man to be unsuccessful in carrying out his mission. Aaron, we're here to offer you protection until we complete our investigation and bring everyone involved in this crime to justice," says the agent. Aaron, immediately gets up from his seat asking questions to the agent.

"Do you know who was plotting to kill me?" Aaron asks nervously as his wife Asia begins to cry. The DEA agent speaks up.

"Mr. Williams, we have our suspicions but because of our continuing investigation we are not at liberty to share it at this time. But rest assured, we have our eye on several suspects," says the agent.

"When should I go back to work?" asks Aaron. The agent from the DEA looks at Aaron then at Asia.

"My recommendation is that you do not go back to work until we take all the individuals into custody that are involved in this murder plot. The Chapel Police Department will be doing surveillance around your house throughout the day and night. Until we can link those involved in this plot and arrest them we feel until that time your life is still in jeopardy. We strongly recommend that you stay at home until you hear from us. If you see suspicious or unusual activity around the area call 911 or the Chapel Police. Agreeing to the agent's request Aaron assures them that he will stay home until notified by the authorities. As the agents and police investigators leave, Aaron and Asia become fragile emotionally. Hugging each other and crying, Asia is confused as to why someone would want to kill her husband. Going around the house making sure that all doors and windows are locked, Asia comes back into the family room. Hearing the phone ringing Asia goes over to answer the phone.

"Hello," says Asia. There is a short pause between her greetings before the caller responds.

"Is Aaron there?" asks the caller.

"No he is not here. May I ask whose calling? The caller appearing to be getting irritated of Asia's response muffles his voice.

"I am a friend of Aaron's sister. Tell Aaron that his sister was in a serious car accident and he needs to get down to University Hospital Emergency right away!" says the caller. As the caller hangs up the phone Asia frantically informs Aaron of the call.

"Aaron you just received a call that your sister was in a serious accident and you need to go over to University Hospital Emergency immediately." says Asia. Reacting to the emergency about his sister being injured in a car accident, Aaron immediately goes and gets his car keys and starts toward the door. Asia goes over and blocks the door causing Aaron to get upset.

"Asia, what are you doing? I got to go!" says Aaron screaming at her. Pleading with her husband, Asia physically pushes him back away from the door.

"Aaron, I think this is a set up to get you over there to kill you! Please call Regina on her cell phone!" she pleads with Aaron. Aaron, still upset with Asia attempts to call his sister on her cell phone and gets no answer. Walking back to the door Aaron begins to physically push Asia out of the way.

GUILTY IS NOT ENOUGH

"Asia, get out of my way!" says Aaron. Asia screams at Aaron upset.

"Call the police! Call the police! Have them come pick you up! I love you! I just don't want anything to happen to you baby!" says Asia getting very emotional. Aaron, heeding to Asia's advice reluctantly calls 911 for assistance.

"911 may I help you?" says the Operator. Aaron, shouting into the phone speaks.

"I need an officer to 35408 Cherry Blossom Lane. I received a call about that my sister who was in a serious accident but I can't go because my wife thinks that this is a setup to kill me! My name is Aaron Williams and the officers were just here. I really need an officer over here now please" he says before giving the phone to his wife. The Operator hearing the urgency of Aaron's call dispatches an officer to the Williams' residence. The dispatcher calmly speaks to Aaron or whoever is on the phone.

"I am sending an officer to your residence. Stay on the phone with me until they arrive," says the Operator. Moments later two officers arrive at the Williams' home responding to the call of someone calling about Aaron's sister being injured in a serious car accident. Inviting the officer in the house Asia explains the details of the call to 911. The officer aware of the planned murder plot probes Asia for more information.

"Did you recognize the voice of the caller?" asks the police officer. Asia looking the officer in the eye responds back nervously.

"No sir, I never heard the voice before. He had a deep voice and seems to have been trying to muzzle it with his hand," she says. The officer gets on his radio to explain the situation with his Commander on duty. After a brief conversation the commander and officer devised a plan to thwart a possible murder attempt to harm Aaron. Calling Aaron and Asia together the officer explains the plan that the commander wants to execute. The officer looks at Aaron and puts his hand on his shoulder.

"Mr. Williams we would like for you to drive your car to the hospital's emergency room parking lot. In the meantime, we will have two unmarked police cars follow you in surveillance for anybody in the vicinity. At the hospital the commander will have officers positioned in detail to protect you if this is a plan to get you to the hospital to attempt harm you. What makes this seems like a murder plot is that our 911 management system hasn't received a call about an accident involving a female in the last twelve hours. In addition, our paramedics haven't reported transporting anyone involved in an accident over the last two hours. What I want you to do is go to your car and follow the lead unmarked car to the hospital. I will be in direct communication with you on your cell phone. Mrs. Williams if you can stay here while we carry this plan out we would appreciate it," says the officer. Upset that she can't be with her husband Asia replies.

"Officer I want to be with my husband. He needs me to be with him!" says Asia. Understanding her plea of wanting to be with her husband the officer responds.

"It's in you and your husband's best interest that you don't come along at this time," says the officer. As Aaron heads down the freeway with several unmarked police cars behind him, he nears the hospital exit. Taking the exit to the light Aaron makes a left turn. Realizing that the hospital emergency parking lot is only two blocks away he starts to get very nervous. Realizing that he has protection around him Aaron slowly turns into the emergency parking entrance where a bright red sign greets him. As he began to park his vehicle he notices a burgundy Honda Civic pulling up next to him. Immediately the unmarked police cruisers converge in all directions on the vehicle with their guns drawn pointed at Joe, the hit man hired by Kimberly to murder Aaron.

"Get your damn hands on the steering wheel and don't move!" says the officers. In compliance to the officer's command, Joe sits there in a moment of paralysis fearing that he will be shot from one of the six weapons pointed at his head. Escorting Aaron away from the scene to avoid any more trauma the officers' snatches open the driver's side door. Pulling Joe out of the vehicle onto the ground, the officers puts him in handcuffs. The shift commander gets a visual identification of him and

GUILTY IS NOT ENOUGH

instructs his officers to place him in the squad car and transport him to the interrogation room at headquarters. The commander then goes over to Aaron who is deeply emotional and exasperated and places his hand on his shoulder. After the arrest is made the Police Commander comes over to Aaron's vehicle and speaks to him.

"Mr. Williams thanks for your cooperation. I know it wasn't easy but I think we solved this murder plot that I know had you and your family on edge. You can leave as soon as we take a few pictures of your car next to the suspects' car as evidence for our crime scene unit. I know you want to get back home to your wife," says the Commander. Leaving the scene Aaron immediately calls his wife crying as soon as she answers the phone.

"Baby, baby I'm okay, "says Aaron crying as he talks. As Aaron slows down driving fearful that he is going to have an accident because of his emotional state, he cries as he continues to speak to his wife.

"Asia, I almost got killed!" says Aaron. Trying to explain the details to his wife and getting more verbally emotional, Asia realizing the risk interrupts her husband's conversation.

"Aaron, please drive home safely, we will talk about it more when you get here, okay?" she says pleading with him. After complying with his wife's request, Aaron ends his call and continues to drive safely home. Moments later Asia receives a return phone call from Pastor Wright. After several rings Asia answers Pastor Wright's call.

"Hello Pastor Wright.

"Hello Asia, I was returning your phone call," he says.

"Yes, I was calling you about an emergency we had but everything is alright now. We would like to share with you the details of all that happen later," says Asia. Pastor Wright informs Asia that he will stop by later. As soon as Asia hangs up the phone with Pastor Wright, her husband Aaron pulls into the driveway. As Aaron gets out of the vehicle Asia immediately goes out to greet him. As she embraces him and gives him a very romantic kiss, they walk back into the house while embracing each other.

"Aaron, I was so afraid that you wouldn't make it home. I even called Pastor Wright who said he will be over. As Asia embraces Aaron tightly, Aaron smiles and gives her a kiss. As they walk inside the house into the family room and take a seat, Aaron takes a deep sigh of relief. Moments later the doorbell rings causing Asia to leave the family room to see who it may be.

"Who is it?" asks Asia.

"It's Pastor Wright," he says. Quickly opening the door, she greets Pastor Wright with a warm embrace, they walk into the house.

"Thank you Pastor for coming over on such short notice. Aaron is in the family room a little shaken up from his ordeal," says Asia. As she directs him into the living room Pastor Wright makes eye contact with Aaron then walks over and gives him a big hug while whispering in his ear.

"God bless you Aaron," says Pastor Wright. Feeling a sense of calmness in the air, Asia opens up the discussion by thanking the Pastor for coming by.

"Pastor as you know, Aaron and I have been going through some extremely difficult times the past several weeks. You have been so supportive with your spiritual wisdom and prayers. Just when we thought things would get better we received a call today from an individual who said that he was a friend of Aaron's sister. He wouldn't identify himself by name but said that Aaron's sister was in a serious car accident and that he needed to come to University Hospital Emergency immediately. Unsure who the caller was I told them he wasn't here and tried to get him to leave a message. He wouldn't leave one but he had a husky voice that seemed to be muzzled by his hand. Aaron tried to call his sister to no avail which gave him the reason to believe that what he was saying was true. Because of the uncertainty regarding the call, I had Aaron call the police. From here Aaron can tell you what happened after that," says Asia.

Aaron nervously starts his conversation by telling Pastor the final details of his near encounter with death.

"Well Pastor, the 911 Operator informed me that one of their officers was nearby and she would dispatch him over. Through the advice of the police commander they encouraged me to drive to the hospital emergency room parking lot with two unmarked police cars following me. Once we arrived to the emergency room parking lot I saw a Caucasian man in a faded burgundy Honda Civic pulled up next to me. At that point the police swarmed his vehicle with guns out placing him under arrest," says Aaron nervously replaying the scene. Pastor Wright hearing the dramatic accounts of what Aaron went through encourages Aaron and Asia to come closer to him. Taking their hands he asked them to join him in prayer. After a brief prayer the Pastor advises them to stay close to each other and pray daily. Looking at his watch Pastor Wright realizes that he is almost running late for his next appointment gives Aaron and Asia an embrace before leaving.

Chapter 11

Later in the afternoon after being processed at the detention center Joe is brought in brightly lit interrogation room at the justice center. Handcuffed and in his orange inmate's jumpsuit Joe is squirming in his seat trying to adjust the handcuffs that was placed on his wrist tightly. Walking up to Joe demanding answers Detective Lawson stares at him.

"Tell me Mr. Fields who you are operating with?" says the Detective. As the Detective pacing the floor. Joe looks up at the Detective angrily.

"I said nobody!" says Joe. Walking up close to Joe giving him little breathing room he calmly asks his question again.

"Going to ask you one more time. Who are you operating with Joe? Detective, literally gets in Joe's face screaming at him. Twisting in his chair uncomfortable in handcuffs, Joe responds again.

"I said nobody!" says Joe.

"I've been on the force for over thirty years and I know when I'm being lied too! If you want to take the fall by yourself, that's fine. It will be your butt in the slammer!" says the Detective. As the Detective paces around he thinks of another investigated tactic to use on Joe.

"Mr. Fields, I will cut a deal with you. If you tell me who else is involved I will testify in court that you cooperated with us and see that you get very little time in jail. Are you aware that you are looking at possibly twenty years in prison if you are convicted on these charges? However being the caring Detective that I am I'm willing to tell the Prosecutor to cut you a deal if you tell me who else was involved in this murder plot," says the Detective. Joe, still aching in discomfort from the handcuffs laughs at the Detective.

"You must think I'm a fool. You all say that then have me going up the river," says Joe.

"No problem Mr. Fields, have it your way. I will have them take you down to the county jail until your court date," says the Detective. As the Detective starts to leave the Interrogation Room Joe calls him back.

"Okay Detective, what you want to know?" says Joe.

"Who got you to set up the murder plot of Mr. Williams?" says the Detective.

"Kimberly," says Joe.

"Kimberly who?" says the Detective.

"Kimberly Downing," says Joe.

"Where do you know Kimberly Downing from?" asks the Detective.

"She works at the Remington Corporation," says Joe. As the Detective writes down the down of the alleged accomplice in the murder for hire plot, he shares the name with the investigation team to run information on Kimberly Downing. After having Joe processed and taken to the county jail a thorough investigation by the Drug Enforcement Agency and the Chapel Police Department begins. Three days after an intensive investigation, the DEA in coordination with the Chapel Police Department arrested Kimberly Downing, Chief Financial Executive for the Remington Corporation and David Brewer. Downing is charged with complicity to commit murder. Brewer is charged with one count of Illegal Wiretapping. Both are currently detained in the County Jail pending a preliminary hearing. There are other pending charges that are being investigated. As soon as the news of this major development broke, news the media across the country brought it to the attention to the public. When news got to Robert Remington Sr. he refrained from making any comments to the media.

Sitting at home in their family room, Aaron and Asia is watching the evening news when it opens up with breaking news.

"We bring you breaking news from Chapel where Senior Financial Executive Kimberly Downing Chief Financial Officer of the Remington Corporation was arrested by the Drug Enforcement Agency and Chapel Police and charged with complicity to commit murder, aggravated drug trafficking, illegal wiretapping and bank fraud. Two accomplices, Joe Fields and David Brewer were also charged and arrested. We will bring you more developments as we get more information. As the news broke Aaron drops his head and cries as Asia goes over to console him. Shocked of the fact that his professional colleague and co-worker Kimberly Downing was involved in having him murdered.

"I can't believe it! I can't believe Kimberly would do such a thing to me! I know we didn't have a close relationship, but to have me murdered? It doesn't make any sense," says Aaron looking sadly at his wife. As Asia continues to console her husband she gives him a few words of encouragement.

"Baby, at least you are here to talk about it and continue to pray for all of us including the Remington Corporation that we all will come out of it and move forward," says Asia.
Moments later, Aaron's cell phone rings. The call is from Agent Blake of the DEA. Aaron puts the call on the speaker so his wife can hear the conversation.

"Hello," says Aaron.

"Hello, this is Agent Monica Blake of the Drug Enforcement Agency. How are you?" says the agent.

"Okay, I guess,' says Aaron.

"I'm calling you regarding the investigation of the Remington Corporation. I wanted to update you on the status of our investigation. As you may or may not heard, we have made some arrest in the case regarding the crimes committed at the Remington Corporation. Most notably, one of the persons we have arrested is one of your co-workers Kimberly Downing. As we continue our investigation, we will keep you informed of any progress regarding the case. You will also hear it through the media. As far as your employment, I think it's safe to say that you can return to work as scheduled. I would just let your employer know that you have spoken to us and all is clear," says Agent Blake. As Agent Blake and Aaron gets off the phone, Asia smiles at Aaron and continue to give him words of encouragement.

"You see how God has worked things out baby? Within seventy two hours you went from your life being at risk to you being safe and able to return to work. I think I need to call Pastor Wright and share with him the good news," says Asia. As Asia calls Pastor Wright, he immediately answers his phone.

"Hello Pastor Wright, this is Asia Williams how are you?" says Asia.

"I am doing well.

"I am calling you to update you on the situation with my husband. Agent Blake of the Drug Enforcement Agency called about twenty minutes ago and informed Aaron that the other suspects in the case were arrested. And one of those who were arrested was his co- worker by the name of Kimberly Downing, the Chief Financial Controller of the Remington Corporation. She also informed Aaron that it was also safe for him to return to work. Pastor, God has blessed us through this ordeal. And we want to thank you for being there for us in our time of need." said Asia. Hearing Asia share the updated information, Pastor Wright responds.

Asia, God will continue to bless you and Aaron. I will continue to pray for you and Aaron.

Three weeks after the Federal Drug Enforcement Administration served a search warrant on the Remington Corporation, Agent Monica Blake of the Drug Enforcement Agency and a team of law enforcement are assembled in the conference room filled with news media from across the State announce details regarding the Remington Corporation. As DEA Agent in Charge Monice Blake comes up to the podium to start the press conference everyone becomes attentive as she speaks.

"The Drug Enforcement Agency in cooperation announces State, County and Local law enforcement are here to bring you an update on our investigation regarding the Remington Corporation. After much discussion, the federal grand jury of the United States Superior Court has handed down indictments related to our investigation of illegal drug trafficking at the Remington Corporation. As a result of our extensive investigation the following indictments are being released. Indictment One involves Kimberly Downing, Chief Financial Controller of the Remington Corporation of one count of illegal drug trafficking. This criminal activity was administered at the Remington Corporation where Kimberly Downing is employed as their Chief Financial Officer used the corporation to sell and distribute drugs. Indictment Two is one count of illegal wiretapping by where Kimberly Downing is accused of hiring a technician to cross the wires of the phone lines in the Remington Corporation to gain personal and private information of another employee working at the Remington Corporation. Indictment Three is one count of bank fraud by Kimberly Downing. This indictment involves Kimberly Downing making illegal financial transactions using funds of the Remington Corporation for illegal drug operations. And lastly, Indictment Four accuses Kimberly Downing of complicity to commit murder. In this indictment Kimberly Downing is accused of hiring a person of interest to plan and plot a murder for hire of a co-worker at the Remington Corporation. If convicted of all charges Kimberly Downing could face up to 120 years in prison. We will not be taking questions at this time because of our ongoing investigation of this criminal operation," says Agent Blake. Watching and hearing the federal indictments levied against his Chief Financial Officer Kimberly Downing from his office, Robert Remington Sr. was quite disturbed. As numerous calls flooded the phone lines and a host of news reporters arrive at the Remington Corporation, Mr. Remington Sr. refuses interviews and any comments pertaining to the indictments rendered today.

Appearing in U.S. Superior Court for her preliminary hearing before Judge Edith Melton, Kimberly Downing sits in her seat very still. Sitting next to her defense attorney in the cavernous looking courtroom, Judge Melton looks over at the Federal Prosecutor Michael Sweeney as he motions to court personnel that he was ready to start the court trial. As the Case Presenter prepares to read off the charges the courtroom including Kimberly Downing's family and staff as well as the media gets very quiet.

"Let me start by hearing the particulars of the cases," said Judge Melton.

"Before you your honor is the U.S. Superior Court vs. Kimberly Downing on four criminal indictments. On case number 22-1984, Kimberly Downing is charged with one count of illegal drug trafficking. This criminal activity was administered at the Remington Corporation where Kimberly Downing is employed as their Chief Financial Officer used the corporation to sell and distribute drugs. On case number 22-1985, Kimberly Downing is charged with one count of illegal wire-tapping by where Kimberly Downing is accused hiring a technician cross the wires of the phone lines at the Remington Corporation to gain personal and private information of another employee working at the Remington Corporation. On case number 22-1986, Kimberly Downing is accused of making illegal financial transactions using funds of the Remington Corporation for illegal drug operations. On case number 22-1987, Kimberly Downing is accused of hiring a person of interest to plan and plot a murder for hire of a co-worker at the Remington Corporation," says the Case Presenter. After hearing the four charges that Kimberly Downing is accused of Judge Melton addresses Kimberly Downing's Defense Attorney.

"Counsel, how your client pleads to the charges?" ask Judge Melton.

"My client pleads not guilty to all the charges your honor," say Attorney Langford. After making notes on her computer Judge Melton responds.

"I accept the defendant's not guilty plea on all four charges. Now, as it relates to bond for the defendant let me here from the State," says Judge Melton. Prosecutor Sweeney stands up and addresses the Judge.

"Your honor, because of the seriousness of the charges presented to the courts and the fact that we deem the defendant not only a flight risk but the fact that the alleged in the case is in the community and at risk our recommendation is no bond for the defendant," says the Prosecutor. After hearing from the State and making notes, the Judge looks over at the defense table.

"May I hear from defense counsel as it relates to bond," says Judge Melton. Defense Attorney Langford stands up from her seat at her defense table and responds.

"Your honor, my client has been a resident of this county for over twenty-five years. She has property here and doesn't have any past criminal record before the charges other than the charges brought before the courts today. My client is not a flight risk and if given a reasonable bond the defendant will be able to take care of personal matters before her next court trial. Your honor, we are asking for a reasonable bond so my client can arrange her business and personal affairs before the next court date," says Attorney Langford. Taking a moment to ponder what she heard from both counsels Judge Melton makes her decision regarding bond.

"I took into account everything presented by both counsels. I will set bond at five hundred thousand dollars ten percent for the defendant. I will also order that the defendant wear an electronic monitoring unit if released from bond per the courts," says the Judge. As Judge Melton looks over her calendar on her laptop she looks at both counsels.

"Counsels, how does Monday June 17th at 9: 00 a.m. look for you," say Judge Melton. As both counsels looks at their schedule seeing their availability they both acknowledge their availability. Hearing that both counsels are available Judge Melton responds.

"Let's schedule this court trial for Monday June 17, 2022 at 9:00 a.m. with the selection of jurors. So, if there is nothing else before the courts today regarding this case is adjourning until June 17th at 9:00 a.m." says Judge Melton as she leaves the bench and goes to her chambers. As court security places the handcuffs back on Kimberly Downing and takes her to the security room near the courtroom, to return back to the detention facility.

Chapter 12

Three weeks after her preliminary hearing, Kimberly Downing, wearing an orange detention jumpsuit is escorted into the courtroom by court security. She is taken to the defense table and seated next to her defense attorney. As court personnel scurry around getting themselves in place before court is officially in session, the room gets quiet. Moments later the Bailiff gets the attention of everyone in the courtroom.

"Court is in session. All Rise, the Honorable Judge Edith Melton of United States Superior Court presiding," says the Bailiff/ As Judge Melton walks into the courtroom from her chambers to her bench she is greeted by court personnel. Taking her seat, she looks up and speaks to everyone in the courtroom.

"You may be seated. Shuffling through her court papers inserted in her legal file folder Judge Melton looks up at the both counsels and the federal marshals assigned to the court trial.

"Security, please bring the jurors into the courtroom," says Judge Melton. Moments later court security escorts the twelve jurors to their jury box where they all are seated. Judge Melton turns her attention to the jurors.

"Welcome to the U.S. Superior Court. You all have received and were given instructions regarding your responsibilities as a juror in this trial. With that being said, I would like to start this trial with opening statements from the Prosecution," says the Judge. As Prosecutor

Michael Sweeney gathers his legal papers and leaves the table, he goes to the front of the courtroom and presents his opening statements.

"Before the court this morning is the defendant Kimberly Downing, indicted on the following charges. One count of illegal drug trafficking, one count of illegal wiretapping, one count bank fraud and one count of complicity to commit murder. After receiving information regarding of a illegal drug trafficking operation at the Remington Corporation. As a result of the information, the Drug Enforcement Agency started an investigation. That investigation led to a court ordered search warrant at the Remington Corporation. Seized were two telephones, two voice mail systems and several boxes of documents related to the investigation. This evidence led to charges being filed and grand jury indictments by the Drug Enforcement Agency. As a result, defendant Kimberly Downing was arrested and charged," says the Prosecutor. As Prosecutor Sweeney goes back to his table, Judge Melton turns her attention to the defense table to Attorney Langford.

"May I hear opening statements from defense counsel," says Judge Melton. Attorney Langford quietly speaks to her client before walking to the front of the courtroom.

"As I represent my client Kimberly Downing regarding the cases before you in this court trial, I will be able to present details of what wasn't presented by the prosecution. It is related to my client's mental condition at the time of these criminal offenses before you today. Six months ago, my client Kimberly Downing was romantically involved with a man name Tony. As they became more romantically involved, my client was introduced recreationally to cocaine. As the relationship grew, my client became addicted to cocaine. Because of her addiction, she became less efficient on the job, making poor decisions in judgment, having severe mood swings, running into personal financial problems and yes, started having cocaine withdrawals. My client found out later in their relationship that her boyfriend was part of a drug trafficking ring transporting drugs from Mexico to the United States. He demanded that my client use the Remington Corporation as a cover for his drug operation to hide money. When my client first spoke against it he threatened to harm her if she didn't cooperate. As all this was going on my client became paranoid that a co-worker by the name of Aaron Williams was attempting to take over the Remington Corporation after getting the corporation to Fortune 500 Status. Noticing that Aaron Williams was getting a great amount of attention and the President and CEO of the Remington Corporation could not see or accept the takeover that was happening. My client, because of her concern to protect and the corporation decided to contact a friend who had a friend who was a phone technician. He knew how to have it where my client could track phone calls attempting to take over the Remington Corporation. After connecting with the technician, my client soon discovered through a mistake that he mistakenly crossed lines, having her voice messages going to her co-worker's voice messages. My client immediately went to the corporation's Receptionist to inquire about her phone calls. After the Receptionist discovered that my client's phone calls were going to Mr. Williams' office phone, she went to retrieve her calls. Not only did my client get her calls she realized messages of drug distribution and drop off at the Remington Corporation was sent by her ex-boyfriend she broke up with. In a state of panic and temporary insanity realizing that he knew of the drug operation and she would be implicated in a drug trafficking operation my client decided to hire someone to have Mr. Williams killed to hide the evidence. Our not guilty plea by reason of temporary insanity is based on the fact that my client at that time was addicted to drugs, and made decisions not in the proper state of mind. Realizing what she had done and knowing that she needed clinical help sought help from a local Psychologist, Dr. Richard Livingston. Your honor, I would like to bring to the witness stand Dr. Livingston to share with the courts his evaluation as it relates to my client Kimberly Downing," says Attorney Langford looking at the Judge. Taking a brief moment to consider counsel's request Judge Melton responds.

"At this time Dr. Livingston can take the witness stand regarding the defendant," says Judge Melton. As Dr. Livingston promptly leaves his seat and approaches the front of the courtroom next to the witness stand.

"Do you swear to tell the whole truth nothing but the truth so help me God?" asks the Bailiff.

"I do," says Dr. Livingston. As Dr. Livingston takes a seat in the witness stand he is approached by Attorney Langford.

"Good Afternoon Dr. Livingston. On April 4, 2022 did you have any contact with a Kimberly Downing?" as Attorney Langford.

"Yes," said Dr. Livingston.

"Do you see Kimberly Downing in the courtroom today?" asks the attorney.

"Can you identify Kimberly Downing at this time?" says Attorney Langford.

"Yes, she is sitting at the table wearing the orange outfit in the front row," says Langford.

"On April 4th when you were seeing my client, at what capacity was she being seen?' asks Langford.

"Ms. Downing was seen clinically for severe depression after having episodes of trauma at her place of employment," says Dr. Livingston.

"Dr. Livingston, can you expound more regarding the problems at her place of employment?" asks Langford.

"The patient shared much of what you said earlier of her past romantic relationship, the drug operation she was forced to be involved in and a co-worker who was attempting to take over the corporation" says Dr. Livingston.

"After clinically evaluating my client Kimberly Downing what was your clinical diagnosis?" asks Attorney Langford.

"I diagnosed her with acute stress disorder which is a short term mental health condition that can occur within the first month after experiencing a traumatic event. It can include Anxiety, intense fear or helplessness, flashbacks or nightmares, feeling numb or detached from one's body, along with avoiding situations and having homicidal and suicidal tendencies," says Dr. Livingston.

"So Dr. Livingston, in your clinical opinion did you see my client suffering from any and all of these conditions?" asks Attorney Langford.

"Yes," says Dr. Livingston.

"Dr. Livingston are any of those conditions would be suicidal and homicidal ideation?" asks Attorney Langford.

"Yes," says Dr. Livingston. After hearing Dr. Livingston's response Attorney Langford turns her attention to the Judge and responds.

"Your honor, that's all I have for the witness," says Langford. As the attorney goes back to her seat at the defense table, Judge Melton looks over at counsel.

"Cross examination from the State?' ask Judge Melton. Prosecutor Sweeney slowly gets up and responds as he walks toward the witness stand.

"Yes your honor," says the Prosecutor. As Prosecutor Sweeney walks closer to the witness stand and stares at the Psychologist.

"Dr. Livingston, at any time during your interview and clinical evaluation did the defendant Kimberly Downing mention anything to you about the murder for hire plot that she was involved in?" asks Sweeney.

"No she didn't," says Dr. Livingston. Prosecutor Sweeney immediately looks at the Judge and responds.

"That's all I have your honor," says the Prosecutor. After hearing the Prosecutor, Judge Melton looks over at the witness stand.

"Dr. Livingston, you may leave the witness stand," says the Judge. As Dr. Livingston leaves the witness stand returning to his seat. Keeping the court trial moving along Judge Melton after typing in notes looks over to the Prosecutor.

"Does the State have anything before we go to closing arguments?" says Judge Melton. Prosecutor Sweeney immediately stands up and addresses the Judge.

"Your honor, the State would like to bring to the stand two witnesses who can share what they know regarding the charges against the defendant Kimberly Downing. First the State would like to bring to the witness stand Michael Fields," says Prosecutor Sweeney. Acknowledging the State's request Judge Melton responds.

"Michael Fields may take the stand," says the Judge. As Michael reaches the witness stand and is sworn in he takes a seat. As Prosecutor Sweeney walks closer to Michael Fields he greets him.

"Good afternoon Mr. Fields, can you tell the courts what you know about the charges before the court and your involvement," says Sweeney.

"Yes, I was contacted by Kimberly Downing'" says Michael Fields. Hearing that Prosecutor interrupts him and responds.

"Mr. Fields, do you see Kimberly Downing in the courtroom?" asks the Prosecutor.

"Yes, she is wearing the orange jumpsuit sitting on the front row," says Michael.

"For the record, the witness Michael Fields has identified the defendant Kimberly Downing, You may continue," says the Prosecutor

"Well, Kimberly Downing contacted me asking if I would do a job for her. That job was to do a murder for hire on her co-worker at the Remington Corporation which I agreed. We met at the Mario's Italian Restaurant to further discuss plans for me to do the job. We agreed on a price and location to commit the murder which was the Pyramid Tower Garage. Unfortunately, her co-worker did not show up which caused me to leave. Later that day Kimberly Downing and I devised a plan where I would call her co-worker Aaron Williams and tell him that his sister was in a serious accident and he need to get down the emergency room parking lot at University Hospital where I was going to meet him and murder him. Unfortunately for me when he arrived he had two unmarked police cars around him. When I was getting ready to get out of my car two officers approached me with guns out and placed me under arrest. They took me to headquarters and interrogated me regarding my involvement in the crime. After intensive questioning I informed them that I was working for Kimberly Downing who put me up for this murder for hire. As part of a plea bargain I agreed to testify against her," says Michael. As Michael Fields finishes his testimony

Judge Melton states that he can leave the witness stand. Moments later Prosecutor Sweeney looks at the Judge and speaks.

"Your honor, the State would like to bring to the witness stand Aaron Williams," says Sweeney. Judge Melton responds immediately.

"Aaron Williams may take the witness stand, "says the Judge. As Aaron slowly gets up from his seat in the rear of the courtroom he embraces his wife before walking to the front of the courtroom to the witness stand where he is met by the Bailiff.

"Do you swear to tell the whole truth nothing but the truth so helps me God?"

"I do," says Aaron Williams. As Aaron takes a seat in the witness stand Prosecutor Sweeney walks toward him and starts his dialogue.

"Mr. Williams, it is the court's understanding that you were a victim in some of the charges related to this court trial. It is also our understanding that you worked with the defendant Kimberly Downing at the Remington Corporation. If you can share with the court your experience as it relates to this case as well as your relationship with the defendant Kimberly Downing," asks Prosecutor Sweeney. As the Prosecutor goes back to her table Aaron takes a moment to compose himself before addressing the court.

"Well, it all started when I arrived at work at the Remington Corporation the morning of Monday February 7th. After meeting with the President and CEO Robert Remington Sr. about my successful bids to get the Remington Corporation to Fortune 500 status. As I was going to Mr. Remington's office I greeted Kimberly Downey who was our Chief Financial Officer. For some reason she did not respond to my greeting or made eye contact with me. Then a week later arriving to work after a weekend off I happened to ask the receptionist have I received any messages to which she replied that I did. When I went into my office I noticed that several lines to my phone were lit up letting me know I had several voice messages. After I sat down and got myself comfortable, I decided to check my voice messages. To my surprise and very shocking was two messages from a unknown source. The first message spoke of an illegal drug trafficking operation involving the Remington Corporation. It talked about a drop off point near the Remington Corporation and the second message mentioned about plans to pick up money at Series Bank, the financial institution where the Remington Corporation has its corporate accounts. Hearing those messages and not knowing who in the corporation was involved in this illegal drug operation caused me have severe panic attacks and I got extremely nervous. I wasn't sure if our President and CEO was involved in this corruption. At that point I started to get very emotionally sick. I immediately called my wife and told her that I was sick and was coming home. Then I got my suitcoat and briefcase, locked my office door and went to the reception area to inform our Receptionist that I have become ill and was going home for today. She was shocked to hear that I was ill because I had only been at work for an hour. While driving home I became confused to what I should do about my new revelation. Do I be quiet and don't say nothing about what I heard on the voice message or be a whistleblower and risk my job or more critically my life if the person involved found out that I know of the illegal drug trafficking operation? When I arrived home my wife greeted me and immediately realized that something else was going on other than an illness. I finally shared with my wife Asia what was going on and she suggested that we talk to our Pastor. After speaking with our Pastor he strongly recommends that we go to the authorities on this illegal operation. In fact, he had a friend who works with the Drug Enforcement Agency and ask if we wanted him to contact her. We agreed and from that he set up a meeting so I could share what transpired at the Remington Corporation. From there the Drug Enforcement Agency started their investigation and I was strongly encouraged to not return to work at this time while they were investigating. It was a good choice because I found out later that there was a murder for hire plot set up to murder me. What was very striking was I later found out through the DEA investigators that the person that has planned my murder was my co-worker Kimberly Downing. The person who was eventually arrested and charged in the murder for hire plot was waiting in the parking garage where I work near my private parking space to kill me when I arrived that morning. Then I found out that the reason why I got those messages is because Kimberly Downing hired a rogue phone technician who accidentally crossed the wires that caused Kimberly Downing's phone messages to come to my office phone. I was so close to not being a whistleblower and who knows how long this operation would be going on. And more critically how many people would have been killed or addicted in our communities. I want to take this time to ask Kimberly Downing why? Why did you want to kill me? I know the verdict in this case will be decided by a jury of twelve and I respect that. And I know that the most one can received for the crimes that Kimberly Downing committed is a verdict of guilty. However, for all that Kimberly Downing caused to me, the Remington Corporation staff, I am under the belief that guilty is not enough, "says Aaron Williams as he breaks down emotionally crying on the witness stand. Realizing the level of the witness' emotions, Judge Melton summoned court security to escort him back to his seat. As things settled down in the courtroom Judge Melton speaks out clearly.

"We will take a twenty-minute court recess and I will ask court security to escort the jurors from the courtroom. I am asking that counsels and the defendant to not leave the courtroom," says the Judge. As Judge Melton leaves the bench to go to her chamber the courtroom becomes silent after hearing Aaron Williams' testimony on the witness stand.

Chapter 13

After a twenty-minute recess Judge Melton leaves her chamber and comes to her bench and resumes the court trial.

"We will resume the court trial of the United States vs. Kimberly Downing. At this time I will ask that court security bring the jurors into the courtroom," says Judge Melton. As court security escorts the jurors into the courtroom and into their jury box Judge Melton resumes the trial.

"I want to begin this court trial with closing arguments with the State. As Prosecutor Sweeney slowly gets up from his table and approach the jurors, he delivers his closing arguments.

"Members of the jury, you heard the definitive testimony of a key witness in this case. You heard from the victim Aaron Williams, a promising executive at the Remington Corporation who testified that he went through the most perilous experiences as a corporate whistleblower. A high ranking executive who made a decision to share of wrong doings going on in the corporation that could have affected numerous people within the corporation and in the community. By doing the right thing which we encourage to protect the legal system he almost was murdered. The fact that he didn't show up for work that day is the reason why he could be here today as a key witness to share his experiences. The defendant Kimberly Downing defense was that she was in a bad romantic relationship and that she was chemically addicted to the drug cocaine when all these crimes occurred. If this were the case why did she wait until she was arrested and charged by the Drug Enforcement Agency to share all this information regarding her addiction and her alleged drug dealer? The prosecution has little to no empathy for the defendant Kimberly Downing and recommends a lengthy prison sentence. Not only did she do irreversible harm to the community but caused long term issues credibility with the Remington Corporation, while the corporation achieved Fortune 500 status. Not only did she defraud the Remington Corporation of thousands of dollars from their bank account to make drug deals she attempted to have a co-worker murdered in the offense to hide her criminal involvement. Not to mention having the phone lines crossed by a rogue technician so she could tap into what he was doing after he successfully helped the Remington Corporation achieve Fortune 500 status," said Prosecutor Sweeney. She almost destroyed an innocent man's life by the name of Aaron Williams as he was doing the right thing by blowing the whistle on an illegal drug operation. That's all I have," says Prosecutor Sweeney as he returns to his seat. As Judge Melton types information on her computer tablet she looks up in the direction of the defense table.

"Closing arguments at this time from the defense," says the Judge. Attorney Langford slowly gets up from her seat after whispering in her client's ear and walks towards the jurors.

"Your honor and members of the jury, as we sum up this court trial you have heard my testimony as well as the testimony of Clinical Psychologist Dr. Richard Livingston regarding my client Kimberly Downing mental and emotional state during the time of the charges brought against her. Dr. Livingston stated that my client Kimberly Downing appear to be suffering from acute stress disorder which is a short term mental health condition that can occur within the first month after experiencing a traumatic event. It can include anxiety, intense fear or helplessness, flashbacks or nightmares, feeling numb or detached from one's body, along with avoiding situations and having homicidal and suicidal tendencies. This is an individual who has no previous criminal history and is well educated. My client Kimberly

Downing has a bachelor's degree in Accounting and a master's degree Finance. In closing, my client was suffering with a severe mental illness at the time of the offenses. We are asking you as jurors to take under serious consideration while reaching your verdict you consider my client Kimberly Downing not guilty by reason of temporary insanity. That's all I have your honor and members of the jury," says Attorney Langford as she goes back to her seat at the defense table to speak quietly with her client. As the court trial ends Judge Melton follows up by speaking to the jurors before sending them out of the courtroom to begin deliberations.

"Members of the jury, you have heard the case of the United States vs. Kimberly Downing. As you prepare to go into deliberations I ask that you only based your decision on the testimonies and the facts brought forth in this case. Please do not use outside information from this courtroom to make your decision. I have instructed the jury foreperson that I can be contacted through court personnel if there is a question related to this case for clarification of a judicial procedure. So, unless there are no other questions before me I will ask that court security escort the jurors to the jury room to begin their deliberations," says Judge Melton. As court security escorts the jurors out of the courtroom to start deliberations Judge Melton leaves the bench to her chambers.

Chapter 14

After four hours of deliberations by the jurors, the jury foreperson informs the court security that they have come to a verdict regarding the case. As the Judge's court administrator informs Judge Melton that the jurors have come to their decision. As both counsels, court personnel, court security and media is notified of the verdict has been reached and the time of the court hearing announce the verdict. As it gets closer to four o'clock and the courtroom starts to get crowded the Bailiff looks around the courtroom preparing to bring the court to order. As the defendant Kimberly Downing is brought into the courtroom by court security and seated next to her attorney the Bailiff brings the court to order.

"Court is now in order. Please rise, the Honorable Judge Melton presiding," says the Bailiff. As Judge Melton comes back into the courtroom and takes her seat on the bench she addresses the court.

"Court is now in session. The jurors in the case of the United States vs. Kimberly Downing has reached their verdict. I will ask that court security bring jurors into the courtroom at this time," says Judge Melton. Moments later, the twelve jurors are brought into the courtroom and taken to the jury box as they sit silently as the Judge speaks to the jurors.

"Before each of the charges and the verdicts are read I want to take time to thank you for your time and service to the community. When you are officially excused from your jury responsibilities I ask that you

GREG STALLWORTH

be very cautious as to whom you share information to regarding this court trial. With that said, I will read each case number and the charges. Then I will ask that the jury foreperson respond by giving the court your verdict on each of the charges," says Judge Melton. As Judge Melton makes notes on her computer she turns to the jury and began her comments to the jury foreperson.

"Will the jury foreperson give the court personnel a copy of the verdict to give to me," says Judge Melton. As the verdict is handed to the Judge and she reviews it briefly she starts the verdict process.

"On case number 22-1984, the United States vs. Kimberly Downing charged with one count of illegal drug trafficking what is your verdict?" asks the Judge.

"We, the jury find the defendant guilty as charged," says the jury foreperson. As the guilty verdict is read Kimberly is seen dropping her head between her hands in disappointment.

"On case number 22-1985, the United States vs. Kimberly Downing charged with one count of illegal wiretapping. What is your verdict?" asks the Judge.

"We, the jury find the defendant Kimberly Downing guilty as charged," says the jury foreperson.

"On case number 22-1986, the United States vs. Kimberly Downing charged with one count of bank fraud. What is your verdict?" asks the Judge.

"We the jury finds the defendant guilty as charged," says the jury foreperson.

"On case number 22-1987, the United States vs. Kimberly Downing charged with one count of complicity to commit murder. What is your verdict?" asks the Judge.

"We, the jury finds the defendant guilty as charged," says the jury foreperson. As all the verdicts are read the Judge concludes the trial by again thanking the jurors for their service to the community. As she releases the jurors from their jury duty asking court security to escort them from the courtroom. Judge Melton then reviews her calendar to determine a date for sentencing. As she gets the attention to both counsels, she shares her sentencing date.

"I want to schedule a date for sentencing on July 17th at ten o'clock. Counsels, are you both available on July 17th at ten o'clock a.m.?" asks Judge Melton. Both counsels look at their calendars and confirm that they are available.

"The defendant will have continued to be held with no bond in the detention center pending our upcoming sentencing. So unless there is nothing else before the court, this hearing is adjourned until sentencing. Judge Melton immediately leaves the bench and goes to her chambers. As court security takes defendant Kimberly Downing to the courtroom security room to be transported back to the detention center.

One month after being found guilty on all four charges in the United States Superior Court, Kimberly Downing is preparing to hear the sentencing by Judge Melton. The courtroom is crowded including local and regional press to hear the sentencing of defendant Kimberly Downing. As the defendant sits next to her attorney the court Bailiff brings the court to order.

"Court is now in session with the Honorable Judge Edith Melton presiding," says the Bailiff.
As Judge Melton walks into the courtroom from her chambers and goes to her bench she reviews her notes before addressing the court.

"We are now at the sentencing phase of the case of the United States vs. Kimberly Downing. Before I impose sentencing, I would like to share a few words with the defendant Kimberly Downing. In all my years as a Superior Court Judge, this case was so intriguing to me. A professional in your position as a Chief Financial Officer for a nationally known corporation I found it difficult to understand why you would be so corrupt. I understand that you mentioned in your testimony that you became addicted to drugs. The President and CEO of the Remington Corporation gave you complete control of the company's finances. And you chose to hide a drug trafficking operation through the corporation's finances. Then when things went wrong when the phone wires at the

Remington Corporation was crossed, your illegal drug operation was exposed. When you found out that a colleague of yours by the name of Aaron Williams had information that he may take to law enforcement as a whistleblower, you arrange for him to be murdered. Then you hid financial profits from the drug trafficking operation under the finances of the Remington Corporation. Your illegal actions almost got Robert Remington, President and CEO of the Remington Corporation under legal scrutiny," says the Judge. Judge Melton takes a brief pause to compose herself before continuing with the sentencing of Kimberly Downing.

"On the following charges, I am composing these sentences. On the charge case number 22-1984 illegal drug trafficking I am sentencing you to twenty years in the custody of the State Correctional. On the charge of case number 22-1985 of which you were found guilty of illegal wiretapping I am sentencing you to eight years in the custody of the State Correctional facility. On case number 22-1986 on the charge of bank fraud you are being sentenced to twelve years in the custody of the State Correctional. And on the charge of 22-1987 complicity to commit murder, I am sentencing you to eighteen years in the custody of the State Correctional. All these sentences will be served concurrently. And as we end this sentencing phase of this most difficult court trial, I can quite honestly say to the defendant Kimberly Downing created crimes that were despicable and ruthless. Your ability to cause these ruthless acts of criminal activities is beyond approach. To bring others into your criminal acts while you held a corporate position at the Remington Corporation is beyond my comprehension. For that, I can say that beyond my judicial boundaries for the charges that you was found guilty of and committed, I feel that the verdicts that guilty is not enough!" says Judge Melton as she immediately leaves the bench and goes to her chamber as court security handcuffs Kimberly Downing and takes her to the security room to be processed and transported to the detention center until she is sent to the Department of Corrections facility to serve out her lengthy prison term

Chapter 15

Two weeks after a very emotional court trial that found Kimberly Downing guilty of all charges, Robert Remington Sr. is holding a special retirement dinner ceremony. This ceremony, announcing his retirement from the Remington Corporation after 40 years. Guest in attendance include the Remington Corporation Board of Trustees, employees and their guest as well as the local media. After an enjoyable dinner and social hour Mr. Remington prepares to hold a press conference. Standing at the podium, Robert Remington Sr. gets the attention of everyone before speaking. Adjusting the microphone he greets the guest.

"Greetings and good evening. I again. Welcome you to the Remington Corporation's 40th Anniversary and Retirement Ceremony. I have several major announcements that I want to share. One, is already known. That is that effective immediately I am retiring after forty years as President and CEO of the Remington Corporation," says Remington Sr. Flanked by his board President and Aaron Williams, with all the local media present, Mr. Remington Sr. continues his speech.

"I am also here to announce my successor for my position of President and Chief Executive Officer of the Remington Corporation. Today, I want to introduce you to our next President and CEO of the Remington Corporation, Mr. Aaron Williams. Mr. Williams formerly held the position as the Senior Account Executive with the Remington Corporation. As the Senior Account Executive, Aaron secured over one hundred million dollars in bids for the Remington Corporation. His bid acquisitions for the Remington Corporation earned the Remington Corporation the prestigious Fortune 500 Foundation Award as one of the most successful financial corporations in the United States. At this time, I would like to welcome you to our next President and CEO Mr. Aaron Williams, says Robert Remington Sr. As Aaron walks up to the podium, he looks out at the guest seated at the tables and smiles. He gives a moment for the applause to decrease before speaking.

"Good evening! As Mr. Remington Sr. said my name is Aaron Williams, and I am very excited to be here as the next President and CEO of the Remington Corporation. Continuing the rich successful history of the Remington Corporation is my ultimate goal as the new President and CEO. To be in position to take a leadership role has been my primary goal since I started employment at the Remington Corporation. Along with Mr. Remington Sr., I want to also thank the board of directors at the Remington Corporation for giving me this opportunity to advance in this corporation. I also would like to thank my wife Asia and my spiritual leader Pastor Wright for encouraging me along the way in my professional journey. But before I take any questions from the media I have a special announcement to make as well. After consultation with Mr. Remington Sr. and the Board of Directors, I have decided to hire a professional business major to replace a former employee who was our Chief Financial Officer. This individual has a master degree in Finance at Harvard University. He is very familiar with the Remington Corporation, even though he has never worked there. When the Remington Corporation decided to hire me as their next President and CEO, I immediately interviewed him, not once but several times. Each time I was very impressed with his professional charisma. So this evening, I want to introduce you to our next Chief Financial Officer of the Remington Corporation, Mr. Robert Remington Jr." says Aaron Williams. With the guest in attendance hearing the name, they immediately stood up and gave Robert Remington Jr. a rousing standing ovation. Robert Jr. gets up from his seat and walks up to the podium and gives Aaron and his dad a hug before going up to the podium to speak.

"Good evening! It's difficult to express my true feelings this at this time. This honestly is a dream come true. Six years ago I left this community to attend Harvard University to receive my master's degree in finance and return to work at my father's company. Well, this evening my dream has come true. It has been a long journey but I made it. I want to take this time to thank God. I also want to thank Mr. Aaron Williams for having the confidence in me and my talents to bring me onboard with the Remington Corporation team to continue its business success. But most importantly, I want to thank my dad for never giving up on me, even during my difficult times. It's time when I let him down by my actions, however he saw enough in me to give me a second chance. With that, I want to openly tell Robert Remington Sr. that I love you and I promise I will continue his legacy through the Remington Corporation. I also want to thank my mom Sarah and sister Deena for their support during my trying times. And thank you to the Board of Directors for my acceptance," says Robert Jr. As Robert Remington Jr. walks away from a thunderous applaud from the guest, he goes over and gives his dad a warm embrace before taking a seat at the table. As things get settled, Aaron Williams walks back up to the podium to finalize the ceremony program.

"And now I will open up the event for questions from the media," says Aaron. As Aaron smiles and looks over the guest he notices numerous hands up from reporters ready to ask questions.

"Yes, the lady in the red dress," says Aaron.

"Yes, my name is Juliann Waiters from Channel 64 Chapel. I know that over the last month there has been challenges for the Remington Corporation from a legal prospective. Can you share with everyone here how your corporation was able to get through this legal storm?" she asks. Aaron looks directly at the reporter and responds.

"First, I want to thank God for getting us at the Remington Corporation through that most difficult time you called a legal storm. I also want to thank our then President and CEO Robert Remington Sr. for believing in us at the Remington Corporation when the media presented what they believe was factual evidence that what was reported was bigger than life when it was just one employee. He encouraged us and kept the corporation going successfully through it all and I thank Robert Remington Sr. for never giving up on us," says Aaron. Pointing in the direction of a reporter wearing a blue sports coat to the left.

"Tim Donahue of the Gazette Free Press. Mr. Williams, it has been highly publicized that you were identified as the Corporate Whistleblower at the Remington Corporation. What was that experience for you when it got out that you shared of criminal wrongdoing at the corporation?" he asks.

"Obviously, it was a shocker to me that something like that was happening in our corporation. However, I knew that if I didn't report it the problem would be so damaging for the Remington Corporation, its reputation and the professional staff who worked there. So I chose to take risk for the best interest of the corporation," says Aaron. Fielding one more question, Aaron points toward the man sitting toward the right side of the room in the brown shirt.

"Thomas Score, Centennial Press Channel 43. You being a black man as I am from a reputable company, did you face racism at any time during the time you were identified as the person who went to the authorities with the criminal information?" says the reporter.

"Believe it or not, I never had a problem with racism as a result of coming forward with the information of criminal involvement at the Remington Corporation except for the person that it involved," says Aaron. Aaron ends the event by thanking everyone for attending the ceremony.

Closing Epilogue

Whistleblowers in America is the single most effective source of information in detecting corporate fraud. According to a 2007 study by PricewaterhouseCoopers focused on economic crime: While professional auditors were only able to detect 19% of the frauds on private corporations, whistleblowers exposed 43%. Executives surveyed estimated that the whistleblowers saved their shareholders billions of dollars. Over the past two decades, a series of financial crises and corruptions have led the U.S. Congress to pass a series of laws aimed at protecting the private sector whistleblowers and incentivizing them to come forward. These laws recognize that internal controls alone are insufficient, and they have significantly increased the regulation of corporations and the financial industry. Employees working at public and private corporations now have some of the best whistleblower protections afforded to any employees. Under most of these laws, whistleblowers are now able to come forward with information confidentially and are covered by anti-retaliation provisions. Whistleblowers are also eligible to confidentially and are covered and also eligible to receive a percentage of government recoveries from successful prosecutions under modern reward laws like the Dodd-Frank Act. Importantly, these modern reward laws have broad transnational applications, so protections and rewards also apply to whistleblowers outside the U.S. These protections and rewards apply even to whistleblowers have a confidentiality agreement. A May 2020 decision in the case of Erhaft v. Bofi Holdings concluded that employer confidentially agreements do not supersede federal whistleblower rights.

Made in the USA
Columbia, SC
28 February 2025